Namesake
MARIE HARTE

ELLORA'S CAVE
ROMANTICA PUBLISHING

An Ellora's Cave Romantica Publication

www.ellorascave.com

Namesake

ISBN 9781419963995
ALL RIGHTS RESERVED.
Namesake Copyright © 2010 Marie Harte
Cover art by Syneca.

Electronic book publication July 2010
Trade paperback publication 2011

With the exception of quotes used in reviews, this book may not be reproduced or used in whole or in part by any means existing without written permission from the publisher, Ellora's Cave Publishing, Inc.® 1056 Home Avenue, Akron OH 44310-3502.

Warning: The unauthorized reproduction or distribution of this copyrighted work is illegal. Criminal copyright infringement, including infringement without monetary gain, is investigated by the FBI and is punishable by up to 5 years in federal prison and a fine of $250,000.
(http://www.fbi.gov/ipr/)

This book is a work of fiction and any resemblance to persons, living or dead, or places, events or locales is purely coincidental. The characters are productions of the author's imagination and used fictitiously.

NAMESAKE
৩

Trademarks Acknowledgement
ಐ

The author acknowledges the trademarked status and trademark owners of the following wordmarks mentioned in this work of fiction:

Grateful Dead: Grateful Dead Productions

After the Voids

In the year 2078, Cross Step, Kansas, is home to the Voids. Each twenty feet tall and just as wide, the three large wormholes appeared out of nowhere a hundred years ago. No one knows where they lead, only that unearthly creatures from different worlds pour through them from time to time. Rumor has it a race known as the Dekken are devouring civilizations out in the vast universe, and that if Earth isn't careful, they may be next. But the citizens of Cross Step have more to worry about than mere speculation. Humans have to interact with the chaos of races constantly in conflict with one another. Norms—humans—are forced to deal with Voiders—those who came through the Voids, as well as a mistrustful government and Conduits—humans oddly affected by the Voids. Many of the Conduits are psychic and more than a little bit unusual.

Victoria Fox happens to be stranger than most.

Chapter One
Cross Step, Kansas, 2078
After the Voids

༄

Victoria Fox deflected the blow aimed at her throat and returned a punch to her attacker's solar plexus. The other woman sucked wind and went down on one knee. Not even pretending to play nice, Vicki kicked her in the face with a low-heeled boot and followed up with another kick to her gut.

The pounding techno beat in Rock Hall, Cross Step's most popular nightclub, echoed Vicki's racing pulse. Several people around her broke into applause, conceding her win, and exchanged money. An atmosphere of lawlessness pervaded the place, as evidenced by the other fights encouraged throughout the bar and the free-flowing booze and drugs. The place smelled like stale alcohol, sweat and nerves. She wanted to get the job done and leave. Period.

"Hurry the hell up, Vic." A towering male loomed over her and snarled, "He's in the back. We don't have all night."

Vicki glared at her cousin. "I'm not exactly partying here, Sean. This bitch attacked me."

"Whatever. Come on. It's only a matter of time before the cops show. We need their hassle even less than the new government wackos tagging Voiders."

"Who cares about government wackos?" Vicki knelt and ran her hands over the groaning woman on the floor. She found a dagger hidden beneath the woman's jacket and hid it between the cushions of a nearby booth. "We're not Voiders."

Sean snorted. "Like anyone's going to take the time to check after one look at you."

Vicki joined Sean as they threaded their way through the crowd who'd stopped to watch Vicki and one of Tommy Chen's girls duke it out. "Oh? And you're not my mirror image, but uglier?"

He flipped her off and shoved aside the congratulatory idiots angling for an introduction.

Admittedly, Sean had a point. Over the years since the Voids arrived, eye color in the Morely family had changed from anything resembling that of a Norm — a "normal" human. Starting with her great-grandmother, for whom she'd been named, each generation of Morelys looked more and more alien. Like Sean, Vicki possessed amber eyes so light they looked almost yellow. In the darkness, the damn things glowed. Not normal, not at all.

Then again, what the hell is normal in this freakish city? The nightclub had as many Voiders in it as Norms, much like the city. Cross Step, Kansas, now consisted of Voiders, Norms, and Conduits — people like her and Sean.

Conduits were humans affected by the Voids. Vicki often wondered if there wasn't more to her family's odd history than those gaping black portals, which had appeared out of nowhere over a hundred years ago. Two stories high and half as wide, the black portals were ringed with an eerie blue light. As far back as Great-Granny Victoria, the Morelys had possessed strange psychic abilities and a connection to the universal doorways, which didn't make much sense, since no one — not even the Voiders — could step too near the Voids without getting violently shocked.

"He's back there." Sean pointed toward a locked door guarded by a gorilla of a man. Teddy, his nametag said. "Do your stuff."

Vicki huffed with irritation and moved in for the kill. She stopped a few feet from the bouncer guarding Tommy Chen's inner sanctum. He lost his look of boredom and focused on her with blatant interest.

"Teddy? Not Bear, Bruiser or Handsome?" Vicki asked with a flirtatious smile as they approached. She shrugged, which lifted her shirt and exposed more of her navel than her low-riding jeans and belly-shirt allowed. Predictably, Teddy zeroed in on her belly button before shifting his gaze to her breasts showcased by the red, too-small top Sean had encouraged her to wear.

Told you, her cousin's look seemed to say.

"You're in." Teddy nodded at her. "You're not," he said to Sean.

"No problem. Just walking my cousin to the door. You take care of her for me, okay?" Sean held out a hand.

Though suspicious, Teddy took it. *Sucker*.

Vicki watched with appreciation as Sean put Teddy down in one punch. "Not bad."

"Better than you with Trampzilla back there." Laughter crinkled Sean's eyes. "No doubt word's reached Tommy that you trounced one of his chicks. Three to one says he picks you to fight next."

"No way. We couldn't be that lucky."

They'd been after Tommy Chen for months. The sly Voider always managed to elude them. His illegal fights were the talk of the town and the place to be if a Voider wanted to network. Rumor had it more criminal associations started in places like these than in the alleyways and deserted warehouses around town. The local police force — the Salinas — were running ragged. Seemed as if every night a new group of organized thugs sprang up out of nowhere.

Sean dragged Teddy to the electronic lock, and Vicki tugged Teddy's thumb to the print pad. When the metal door *snicked*, Sean shoved Teddy aside. He pushed the door open and they calmly walked through just before Sean shut the door behind them. Walking past the inner guards on either side of the door, he preceded Vicki into a room full of brawling Voiders and criminal-class Norms.

"I used to have a life outside of otherworld freaks. Tell me again why we agreed to do this," she murmured into Sean's ear when he bent down to hear her over the shouts and ongoing betting. She spied four fighting platforms, three of which were currently occupied.

"Because it's our job? Because S&V Retrievals is the best? Because we just cleared a ton of money to take a certain you-know-what from you-know-who?"

"Could you be more cryptic?"

"I could, but we need to focus here. Now quit the attitude. Even if we weren't working on a Friday night you still wouldn't be doing anything. So don't be pissy with me because you can't get a date."

She glared. "Look, Romeo. Just because I don't get it on with everything in pants doesn't mean—"

"Your last date was more than six months ago. Talk about a dry spell. Hel-lo, Sahara." Sean chuckled until she slugged him in the arm. "Ow. All right, I'll lay off. Keep to the plan. I'll distract his people while you move in. Do what you have to, grab the ring, and we're out of here. Just make sure he forgets who took it."

"Sure thing. Easy." Vicki huffed. "How the hell am I going to rip that rock off his finger if his tongue's down my throat?"

"I didn't tell you to sex him up. Just distract him. Bad enough you're wearing that getup."

"You *told* me to wear something, and I quote, 'provocative'. Hell, I didn't think you knew any words longer than two syllables."

He tugged her along after him. "Funny. Look, just work your mojo, knock him out and grab the ring. Give me the signal when you're done. This place makes me edgy." Sean stopped as if on alert.

She mentally reached out and felt him using his own "mojo". "There he is."

One man sat in a plush chair on a raised dais with his back to the rest of the room. Surrounded by shifty-looking individuals, he fit right in wearing a ripped, sleeveless t-shirt and grunge jeans. But the clothes couldn't camouflage his power. A tall, muscular Asian in his mid- to late thirties, Tommy Chen practically owned the underground sector of Cross Step. Shaggy black hair, an arresting face somewhat obscured by a pair of dark sunglasses and intricate tattoos covering both his forearms lent Chen a dangerous first impression.

According to one of their contacts, the tattoos could take on a life of their own. A definite oddity even in the world of Voiders.

As she stared at him across the loud, crowded room, Vicki had the sense he stared right back at her, but she couldn't be sure. Unlike her namesake, Vicki couldn't tell the future or read minds. Her talent, like Sean's, was much more visceral in nature.

A large, bruised hand settled on her shoulder. "Okay, Vicki. You're next."

Who is this schmuck, and how does he know my name?

"Dammit," Sean swore. It took three guys bigger than the giant next to her to pull her cousin away.

"I'll be fine," she yelled over her shoulder as she was led to Tommy Chen.

Their target. Finally.

Except Chen didn't let her get close enough to touch him. The guard pulled her to within a few feet of him before Chen held up a hand. On his pinkie finger sat the thin black band she'd been hired to retrieve.

"Lovely form, Victoria. And such pretty eyes." He pushed back his shades. Tommy Chen had eyes as black as night and sexy as sin. Up close, he had more charisma and animal magnetism than she would have guessed from the many surveillance photos she'd seen of him. "Winner takes all, baby," he murmured.

Her pulse raced and her nipples tightened.

"What?" Down, girl. Focus on his ring.

Before she could ask him about that alluring scent he wore, the guard dragged her toward the empty stage and tossed her up onto it. She landed on her feet and waited, her fists clenched. The noise in the crowd subsided, and Vicki looked around her at Cross Step's ugly underbelly. *What the hell have I gotten myself into?*

Chen stood, silencing the room. "Ladies and gentlemen, tonight we have a real treat. Vicki Fox has decided to challenge my best girl, Mei Lin, to a match."

The crowd went wild. But where was Mei—

Mei Lin dropped out of nowhere to land a few inches to Vicki's right. Dodging the blow aimed at her face, Vicki fought back, wondering how the hell this grab-and-go assignment had turned into a no-holds-barred grudge match.

Thankfully, as fast as Mei Lin was, she couldn't meet Vicki's speed or agility. Instinctively drawing on Mei Lin's life-force, Vicki grew more powerful. A fighting spirit, her father liked to call her. A Conduit who absorbed energy through touch and heightened adrenaline—active combat. A freak of nature, like Sean.

Mei Lin kicked her in the stomach hard enough to crack a rib.

"That's it." Vicki knew her eyes glowed. Fierce passions tended to brighten her vision. With startling clarity, she saw every move Mei Lin intended to make *before* she made it. Irritated to be in the limelight, that her cousin had put her up to this, and that they still hadn't nabbed Chen's ring, Vicki took her hostility out on her adversary.

Minutes later, she stepped over Mei Lin's bruised but still-breathing body and jumped to the floor. No one stopped her.

"Congratulations, baby. You're my new best girl," Chen said with a chuckle.

Noise erupted in a cacophony of sound.

Chen reached for her even as she reached for him, which startled her.

Snagging her in an unforgiving embrace, Chen took her breath away in a punishing kiss. This man, responsible for half the crime in the city including murder, drug running and thievery, had his lips—and hands—all over her. Damnation, but the bulge prodding her belly felt huge.

Ignoring the disconcerting need to explore said bulge, Vicki twisted the energy snaking between them and caught Chen's forearms.

The flesh beneath her palms shifted with a life of its own, freaking her the hell out.

"Wh-what are you doing?" Chen asked, caught in the mire of power between them.

"I want your ring. Give it to me, baby, and I'm yours," she whispered and nibbled on his earlobe. "All *fucking* night long." She channeled a blast of his own sexual energy back at him, throwing him off balance.

He groaned and stumbled back, still clutching her, much to the amusement of his friends. To all outward appearances, Vicki and Chen were getting it on. As if she'd make it with an über-criminal in front of this sleazy audience.

Chen pulled off his ring and shoved it into her front pocket, digging his fingers down toward her crotch. Annoyed because she liked the feel of him there, she mentally smacked herself upside the head. *I am so getting laid when we finish this job.*

Ripping herself from Chen, Vicki tried to catch her breath. Chen looked like a well-fed cat. His lids were shuttered as he stared at her, his shirt half open, revealing a smooth, muscular chest. The tattoos on his forearms writhed and hissed as he reached for her again.

Hissed? Time to go.

Chen shook his head and flexed his fingers, a puzzled look on his face. His eyes widened in understanding just as a commotion from the other side of the room drew his attention.

"Salinas!" someone yelled. *Cops.*

Sean suddenly appeared at her elbow and yanked her from Chen, but not before pounding a fist into Chen's belly.

Wishing she had done the same, Vicki ran with Sean and the other panicked occupants toward the far exit into the night.

"Were you going to fuck him or what?" Sean huffed with disgust.

"I got the ring. Gimme a break." *I made out with Tommy Chen. Oh my God. I must be out of my freakin' mind.*

More Salinas rounded the corner, what looked like a battalion of them.

"Shit. We need to split up. Keep the ring and go three streets over. I'll meet you at MacT's." Sean jerked them to a stop.

"What—"

The jerk tore back down the street and slammed into three Salinas, taking them down. He waited to draw more of the cops' attention before running off in the opposite direction. Using the distraction, Vicki made several unplanned twists and turns to shake the Salinas still on her trail. Damn if she didn't also recognize a few of Chen's men getting closer.

Darting down a narrow side street, Vicki frantically looked for MacT's. Sean would have to suggest the one place she'd never been. Not that she came into this area much anyway, but in her zest to create a life for herself, she'd begun frequenting the clubs downtown. Twenty-seven, by anyone's standards, was too young to vow eternal celibacy. Vicki couldn't remember the last time she'd had sex with anyone other than her well-used vibrator. No wonder she'd wanted to hump Chen. He was a definite hottie, if one could overlook his psychotic, criminal tendencies.

Swearing under her breath at her stupidity, Vicki spotted what looked like a neon M when she heard footsteps growing closer.

She raced toward the M and shuttled down the set of stairs leading to the almost pitch-black entrance. "Nice ambience, Sean. A mixture of creepy, seedy and...locked door."

Pissed off, Vicki released her anger and anxiety on the lock. A few seconds later, the bolt broke and she turned the knob with ease.

Finally.

Entering, she made a beeline for the darkest corner of the room, taking note of the one and only hallway on the first floor, the billiards in the back of the bar and the stairwell leading to a second floor. She sat with her back to the corner, pleased at the dim lighting keeping her in shadow.

The cozy bar was crowded but not overly so. It smelled of beer and had an almost pleasant tang she couldn't place. The tempo was more sedate, the rock music not too loud. Conversations continued in low tones and then stopped.

Crap. All eyes were *on her.* She'd been too preoccupied upon first entering to notice. A glance showed her that each male in the place looked more beautiful and more savage than the next. *Great, just what I need. Ravagers.* The Voiders looked human enough until they took on the form of their *guer*, their fighting spirit. Werewolves come to life. Strong as hell yet kind of sexy, in Vicki's opinion, unless you had to fight them.

Very few females sat amongst the crowd, and those that were...

Vicki stared so hard her eyes dried.

Against the back wall by the billiards, a seven-foot tall Ravager — in werewolf mode — screwed a half-naked woman in full view of anyone wanting to watch. The dozen other women sitting at tables or booths had a hand or a head between a male's legs, or, in one case, her bare legs spread open wide on the bar, her naked breasts in the air and her head thrown back as one of the fellas went down on her while his buddy ordered a beer next to him.

This wasn't MacT's.

Chapter Two

"What'll you have?"

Vicki swallowed hard and glanced up. A waitress, fully clothed thank God, stood waiting.

The only noises in the bar to be heard were the clinking of the bartender's bottles and the slurping, sucking sounds of sex.

"Scotch. Straight." *Weirdest damn night of my life. And I know weird.*

The waitress nodded and left. To Vicki's relief, conversations resumed. Keeping her head down but her energy at the ready, she decided to wait it out in here as long as she could. Once Chen's people and the Salinas had time to breeze by, she'd leave. Preferably out the back door.

A beer plunked down in front of her.

"Thanks, but I ordered a Scotch..." She trailed off as four men surrounded her small table.

"You're new," the tallest one said.

Vicki nearly swallowed her tongue. Nearly six and a half feet of pure menace studied her like a hungry wolf. Jeans, biker boots and a black t-shirt clung to him like a second skin. He had ice-blue eyes, cropped black hair and an attitude proclaiming him king of the mountain.

His buddies looked just as fierce. Like the rest of the Ravagers in the place, they had a wild, earthy quality. The men flanking the leader had short brown hair and brown eyes that studied her with intensity. The one on the right didn't smile. His eyes darkened as he stared at her. The one on the left looked like a charmer as he assessed what he could see of her past the tabletop. He grinned and rumbled something she couldn't decipher to the fourth man furthest from her.

The lone blond nodded. "She's definitely sitting at *our* table."

"Sorry." Vicki stood to leave and the four took a step closer.

Before she knew it, they'd moved the chairs and table out of the way. Nothing stood between her and them but a few feet of empty space. And no one around them seemed to care.

The tallest one held her beer out to her.

"You know what? You keep it," Vicki said. "Again, my apologies for taking your table." She met his gaze before realizing her mistake. *Shit. Never look them in the eye. Not unless you want to lose a limb.* She quickly glanced away.

"Our table. Right." The blond cut off the small space between him and the wall she'd been eyeing. Her one avenue of escape now denied.

"Um, guys? You're kind of crowding me." One Ravager she might be able to handle. But four who looked like these predators?

"Good." The charmer winked. "My tall friend here is Eric. I'm Logan, the pretty one." The others snorted. "This is Jesse," he said of the intense brown-haired male next to him. "And the blond is Dominic."

She puzzled over the introductions. Maybe they didn't mean to be so threatening?

"And you are?" Eric asked, the rumble of his voice vibrating along her nerves like a physical caress.

Squelching the urge to shiver, she answered, aware of his knowing gaze. "Vicki."

"Vicki." He savored her name. Heat licked at her womb. "How did you get in?"

"Ah," she paused, wondering if she should tell the truth. "I, well..."

The front door burst open to admit Salinas like invading ants. The minute the lawmen understood they'd busted into a Ravager hangout, they tensed and drew weapons. Everyone in the bar froze. "We don't want any trouble here. We're searching for a young woman, five foot nine, long black hair. Yellow eyes."

They're brown, assholes.

"We seen that here?" the bartender asked.

Everyone around murmured denials, no love for the Salinas a common thread among Voiders.

Surrounded by four giants, Vicki felt safe enough from prying eyes. Hell, if everyone decided to screw the Salinas by withholding information, so much the better.

She let out a relieved sigh then noted her four new friends staring down at her with calculating expressions. "What?"

"Your eyes are unique, Vicki," Eric said in a low voice. He cupped her face, his calloused hands warm against her skin. "Salinas," he said over his shoulder. "Why do you want this yellow-eyed woman?"

"She caused a public disturbance at Rock Hall, assaulted two women and three men and stole private property from Mr. Chen."

"Mr." Chen. Great. My luck to get the Salinas on Chen's payroll. Some in the crowd chuckled while others began talking in louder voices.

"What'll it be, Vicki?" Eric murmured.

"Be?" Damn him. She had a bad feeling he was offering a choice she didn't want to make.

"The Salinas or us?"

By us, did he mean... All four of the men surrounding her seethed with energy. She could *feel* the arousal in each of them pulsing like a living thing. The "us" definitely meant all of them, but Vicki didn't have a choice. No way in hell could she go with the Salinas, especially if they meant to send her off with Chen. With these guys she stood a chance — granted, a slim chance in hell — of escaping intact.

"Damn it." Vicki seethed, annoyed their arousal was stoking her own. First Chen, now Ravagers? *Is this my night for Voider love or what?* Swearing under her breath, she yanked Eric to her. Forcing him to bend to meet her mouth, she gave him her answer.

"Nobody here by that description, Salinas," Dominic yelled. "Now get the hell gone."

Other Ravagers seconded the sentiment.

Not sure if they'd left or not, Vicki tried not to succumb to Eric's wild taste. Basic need, raw sex and a long thick cock against her belly took a huge chunk out of her resistance.

He growled and pressed her hard against the wall, no longer accepting her kiss so much as taking charge of it.

The others stepped closer, caging Vicki and Eric together.

He used his whole mouth — tongue and teeth and lips — to turn her world upside down. One minute she'd been kissing him, the next he had his tongue down her throat and his hand on her breast.

No, not *his* hand. His hands were on her waist as he lifted her effortlessly, wrapped Vicki's legs around him and ground against her damp crotch.

Fingers pinched both her nipples with enough pressure to make her gasp.

Eric swallowed her cry as he dry-humped her against the wall. He swallowed her pleas for more, stroked her lips and drew a drop of blood with sharp teeth. The pain only made the pleasure that much sweeter.

"She's burning up," Logan murmured.

Jesse rasped, "I want a taste."

"Not until Prime's done," she heard Dominic say. "And by the look of him, he hasn't had his fill." Dominic laughed, a hoarse sound full of need.

What the hell's a Prime? Dazed at the intense lust swamping her, Vicki tried to break Eric's hold.

He sucked hard at her neck and groaned. "That's it, fight me." He managed a hand down her pants. How, she had no idea. "Oh yeah, you're wet, baby. So fucking ready."

The others panted in time, as if drawing the same breaths.

"Do it now, Prime."

"Fuck her."

"Mark her," Dominic urged, and the others stilled. "*This one.* I feel it."

Lost to common sense, to the fact she was close to having an orgasm in public, Vicki shifted and cried out when a finger suddenly penetrated her.

"Ride it, baby. Come for me," Eric said, his eyes blazing. "That's it."

"I have to go." Somewhere Sean waited for her. She had to get the client that ring. Vicki couldn't have sex in public with four men...four Ravagers, for God's sake.

But reason didn't make a peep as Eric thumbed her clit and thrust another finger inside her, widening her. Vicki was on fire. The hands on her continued to tease, touching her everywhere.

Eric continued to finger-fuck her and whispered, "Take it. Let your pussy swallow my fingers then my dick. I'm doing to ram it up in you. Bathe you in my seed. Then the pack will have you, again and again, until you belong. We'll take good care of you, Vicki. Real good care."

He nipped her earlobe and she shuddered as she came around him. Bucking against his magical fingers, she clawed at him like a madwoman.

"Christ, that's hot," Logan breathed.

"My turn." Eric's eyes glowed, much like hers, she thought dazedly. He removed his hand from between her thighs and fiddled with the snap of his jeans. Then the snap of her jeans.

Her jeans. Over her now-drenched panties.

Blushing, Vicki pushed at his chest and found Eric immovable. The hands on her breasts shoved her to the wall, no longer playing but restraining. Logan and Jesse growled in warning while Dominic monitored it all behind them.

The hell of it all was that Vicki found them arousing when she should have been screaming at them to let her go. Eric shoved at the waistband of her jeans and tangled his fingers in her pocket. When he brushed against the ring there, Vicki froze.

Sean would be waiting, unaware of Chen's infiltration into the Salinas. Worse, Chen might have already grabbed him, wanting his property back. So much for Sean's grand plan to steal the thing in plain sight.

"I have to go," she said. Eric's cock brushed her belly and she shivered. *He is so damn sexy.* "I really have to go."

"Come around me this time," he ordered.

She stared at his lengthening fangs and brilliant gaze. He bent his head to her throat and positioned himself between her folds. *When the hell did my legs let go of his waist? And why are my pants and panties around my ankles?*

Knowing she had piss-poor timing but unable to help it, Vicki took energy from the men around her. Reaching out to touch Dominic, she linked physically to all of them as she absorbed their strength.

With a mighty yell, she let it go.

The four of them flew back through the air as if carried by a tornado. She spared a moment to straighten her clothes and made sure the four of them could move after crashing through several tables, then tore off like a shot out the back exit.

Vicki chastised herself as the Ravagers' incredible arousal still rode her hard. What had she been thinking? And why the hell was this damn ring important enough to stop right before Eric had a chance to push inside her?

Because Norm/Voider relationships don't work. Especially not with sexually charged, aggressive Ravagers. Rumor had it they fucked anything that moved seven days a week, fifty-two weeks a year. *And I turned that down? I must be nuts.*

After putting a good mile between her and that damn bar, Vicki eased up. She must have lost them. Not wanting to chance that they might track her by scent, she grabbed the nearest bus and made her way home, glad she'd long ago listed the place under her grandmother's name. Considering her propensity to find trouble at work, she'd taken her cousin's advice and hidden her home base. Once Sean realized she hadn't made it to MacT's, he'd look for her here.

Inside the roomy townhouse and seated nervously on the sofa, Vicki waited. She was hungry. Her ribs ached and her jeans chafed, uncomfortably moist at the crotch. *I had an orgasm in a Ravager bar with four wolfish Voiders.* Technically three, she corrected herself, since Dominic didn't do much other than guard them and cheer. *Christ.*

Vicki slapped a hand over her eyes and groaned. But as the minutes passed, she couldn't stop thinking about her Ravager encounter...and why she hadn't wanted it to end.

* * * * *

Sean arrived hours later. He shook Vicki awake and turned on the lights. To her relief, he looked none the worse for wear, just harried.

"Where have you been?" she asked around a yawn.

"Out losing Salinas, Chen's thugs and Ravagers." Sean swore and sank down on the couch next to her. "Fucker of night."

"Ravagers?" she croaked.

"Long story." He winced when she nudged his shoulder.

"What happened?"

"Nothing. Look, why don't we get some shuteye and —"

"Sean Ryan Morely, tell me what happened. I was worried sick."

"Yeah, I could tell by the snoring and the drooling."

Vicki automatically wiped her mouth, only to find it dry. "Funny, smart-ass. I did my best, but it's," she paused and squinted at the grandfather clock in the corner, "four a.m. Seriously, are you hurt?"

"Nothing some antiseptic and a rabies shot won't cure," he muttered. He shrugged out of his jacket and removed his shirt.

Raw bite marks reddened his shoulder near his neck. Looking with an inner eye, she thought his energy appeared disturbed. Not wounded, but...different. Sick at the thought Ravagers had done this to him, Vicki hurried to the bathroom and returned seconds later with a medicine kit. Fixing some ointment and a bandage to his wounds, she asked again, "What happened?"

"I managed to shake the Salinas off my tail. Chen's guys were harder, but I avoided them too. Unfortunately, I met up with some old friends at MacT's." He groaned when she pronounced him fixed, rolled his shoulders, then slipped his shirt back on.

"Old friends?"

"I never told you about that pair of Ravager sisters I met a few months ago. Trust me when I tell you they don't like to be told no."

"Yeah, I get that."

At her knowing tone, he frowned. "How about you fill me in on your night? I waited at MacT's for hours. Then the sex sisters showed up and cornered me. I barely escaped in one piece." He wiggled his eyebrows.

"Please. I'm surprised you didn't jump the both of them with promises to 'call them in the morning'." At his scowl, she laughed. "Ah, so that's what landed you in trouble in the first place, hmm?"

"You don't know the first thing about Ravagers. Sex with them is all well and good, but when they want to mark you, run for the hills."

"Why?" Marking was bad? Dominic had wanted to mark her. She still didn't know exactly what that meant.

"Ravagers like to share sex partners."

"I know that. But I didn't think you were into guys."

"You're hilarious."

"Are you telling me their females wanted to share you?" She goggled at the thought.

Two groups of Ravagers lived in Cross Step. The more "civilized" Savages and the unruly Lawless clan, who lived in their animallike form out in the country. The Savages numbered in the thousands, but Ravager females were rare.

Though Sean liked to spread himself around the ladies, frankly, she couldn't see him sharing himself that much.

"I know we haven't dealt much with Ravagers, but come on, Vicki," he said with a snort. "Are you that clueless?"

"About Ravager sexual practices? Yes, so fill me in." *Please. What the hell did I get myself into with those four?*

"All I can say is I'm glad Chen's not a Ravager. Diana's enough to deal with," he muttered.

"Like Chen's not? Need I remind you he's after us since your brilliant plan failed?"

"Only because you didn't whammy him after you got the ring." Sean touched the bandage at his neck and sighed. "I think he's gotten to the Salinas as well."

"I meant to tell you about that. The cops followed me into a Ravager bar, working for *Mr.* Chen."

"A Ravager bar?" Sean narrowed glowing yellow eyes at her, his emotion still running high. "What the fuck did you stumble into when we split up?"

Vicki didn't plan to go into detail. She did her best to skirt around the fact that four Voiders expressed interest in her. "So I blasted them then I left," she ended.

"That's why your energy seems different." He groaned. "We're screwed."

"What? Why? What about my energy?"

"Vicki, tell me all of it. Leave nothing out. It's important."

She swallowed around a dry throat, knowing this wouldn't be good. "After I lost the Salinas, I hid out, like I told you. Except I must have been sitting at these guys' table because they came up to me."

"What guys?"

"Four huge Ravagers."

"Four? Great, a pack." Sean swore under his breath.

"I know what a pack is, genius. A family unit consisting of a lead female and her packmates. Except these guys were all alone."

"They don't always have a female in their family groupings. I've even seen a few packs with non-Ravager females, but it's rare." He paused, his eyes intent on her. "If no one made a stink in that bar, the pack you met must have been Savage. What happened next?"

"They brought me a beer." She stalled, not wanting to discuss sex with her cousin. She stood and paced.

"Vicki, just tell me." He sighed, sounding resigned. "If it makes you feel any better, my run-in with Kate and Diana nearly did me in. Diana's been trying to mark me for some time and I got sloppy. Trust me, two female Ravagers are enough to put *me* down. I can only imagine four males all over you." He grimaced. "Let me rephrase that."

"Yeah, well..." She couldn't help blushing.

"Shit. Did they bite you?"

"No. But one of them talked about marking me, and I think Eric meant to do so before I zapped them."

"This story is getting worse by the second."

"Why? Because they wanted to mark me? That's like taking a girlfriend, right? It's not marriage or anything."

"It's almost worse. Marking is what they do to someone they want to own. No, it's not a slavery kind of thing. It's hard to explain. Look, once they mark you, you might as well say goodbye to any hopes of a Norm boyfriend. The sex is addictive, so I've heard. It's bad enough without the marking," he muttered to himself. "I can't believe you knocked four of them back then ran."

"What? I should have stayed and waited for them to finish what they started?"

"Hell no. But Ravagers love the chase and they prize strength. The fact they wanted to mark you at all is telling. They must have taken a real liking to you. Probably sensed you're a Conduit. From what I can gather, they really like our type, and there aren't that many of us to begin with. Our energy burns brighter than most." Sean paused in thought and his eyes glowed. "Did they fuck you?"

"Geez, that's kind of personal, isn't it?"

"You said they didn't bite you, but sex can be a powerful craving with them."

"For me or for them?"

"For both."

"Well, I... Well." She cleared her throat and glanced away, feeling stupid. Vicki wasn't a prude, but she didn't talk about sex with her *family*. "I had a good time, but I don't know that they did."

Sean wiped a hand over his face. "How did you get home?"

"I ran for about a mile then hopped on the bus."

"That's a start." He stood. "We need to leave. Now. Grab a bag, enough stuff to get you by for a few days. Then we'll swing by my place. Between Tommy Chen and these Ravagers, we're not looking good to finish this case any time soon."

"No kidding. But rest easy. I had Santora pick up the ring. Our client should have it by tomorrow morning, so one problem solved, at least."

"Great. Now we just have to do some major damage control." Sean looked tired.

"Did someone say damage?" Eric growled from the shadows.

Chapter Three

"Hell." Sean launched himself at Eric, taking the offensive. "Vicki, get out of here!" Before Sean could touch Eric, Jesse and Logan tackled him to the ground.

"No way." Vicki stepped forward to help when rough arms grabbed her from behind. She squirmed but couldn't break free, not even when she tried to tap into the male's energy, which she found blocked.

"She's strong, we'll need to hurry," Dominic rasped.

Eric nodded then motioned to someone behind him. Two women raced in. Both were tall and toned, with long dark hair and glittering eyes. The bustier of the two smiled, showing sharp white teeth.

"Sean, I missed you, baby. I guess when you said you'd be back, you meant later tomorrow, hmm?"

Sean cursed and bucked under Jesse and Logan.

"He's a fighter, like her," Jesse said and shoved his elbow into Sean's gut, knocking the wind from his sails.

"Cut it out," Vicki yelled. She used everything in her to shove Dominic back. The Ravagers had prepared well for this meeting. It was all she could do to move the blond giant.

He slammed against the wall while she raced toward Sean. Before she could reach him, Eric intercepted her. His arms were like steel.

"Let me go," she demanded, breathing hard.

"Still fighting. I like that. And so pretty," he said thickly.

"Eric, let me go!" She threw her all into the effort, but weakened from Dominic and from whatever Eric was doing to block her, she tired quickly.

Sean continued to fight while one of the females, Diana or Kate, ripped his shirt off with sharp nails. She yanked one of the bandages off him and bit over the last imprint one of them had left.

"Get off him!" Vicki panted as she tried in vain to reach Sean. That bite. The Ravager was marking her cousin. Not good.

Sean groaned, pulled the woman closer and forced her to kiss him on the mouth. The fight went out of him and the kiss turned embarrassingly carnal.

"Your turn," Eric promised.

They'll own you. Sean's words echoed in her mind. With a last effort, she kicked with her foot and mind as hard as she could.

Eric hissed in pain and doubled over. He lifted his head, retribution glowing like coals in his gaze. He slowly straightened, backing her toward the wall.

Dominic had the back door blocked. Sean and the women lay between Vicki and the front door, and Jesse and Logan were regaining their feet. With no option left, Vicki darted for the stairs. She ran as fast as she could, hoping to lock herself in the bedroom and leave through the fire escape outside her window. Harsh breath on her neck warned her she hadn't been fast enough.

In seconds, a hard body slammed her belly-down onto the bed. Claws shredded her shirt and sharp teeth pierced the juncture of her throat and shoulder. The pain stung, but not as sweetly as the drugging pleasure lighting up her entire body.

His scent told her it was Eric. Raw sex and a sultry, alluring perfume colored the area, made more intense the harder he sucked at the base of her neck.

In seconds she grew wet and her body flushed with desire. She squirmed to feel his erection against her ass.

He reached around to cup her breast and she moaned, caught in his web.

"You belong to the prime," Dominic rasped.

"Let's pick up where we left off," Logan said on a chuckle. "Vicki, wet and wanting, waiting on hard Ravager cock."

Eric finally released her neck. He stripped her bare in seconds, his claws slicing up her clothes without scratching her once. He sucked in a breath. "That ass is mine."

No one objected.

"And that pussy is mine. You're mine, Victoria Fox. All of you."

"Prime's," Logan said.

"Prime's," Jesse agreed.

"Make her pack, Prime." Dominic had the final word.

Eric propped her up on her hands and knees. "Don't move."

Her legs felt like jelly, but she couldn't have disobeyed even if she wanted to. She couldn't understand how, but their energy grew, changing. No longer four separate beings, they felt like one entity. And all of it wanted *her*.

Eric shoved a finger inside her without warning. She groaned as his digit slid in, thick and intrusive, yet without encumbrance. She was so damn wet.

"Good."

Staring down at her midnight blue comforter, she couldn't see Eric. She could only feel him as he nudged her knees apart with his naked thigh. He seemed so solid, so powerful behind her. She'd never in her life felt weak, but next to him and the others, she felt vulnerable as she bent before him.

The fighter in her stirred. She tried to shift away but Eric stopped her by imprisoning her hips, holding her still. He groaned. "That's it. Don't give in, not yet." He teased her with the tip of his cock, thick and solid, as he began to enter her. "This is going to feel so damn good."

"Too bad it's going to have to wait," Dominic growled. "We've got company."

Jesse and Logan swore. Eric shuddered behind her and continued to push until he was balls-deep. They remained locked for a moment, the carnal intensity between them palpable.

"Prime?" Dominic said softly.

"*Fuck.*" Eric slowly withdrew and pulled Vicki to her feet, his arm around her belly as he clasped her back to his chest.

Vicki had a hard time understanding what had happened. Her body was on fire, needing him in the worst way, while her mind shrieked at her to escape. She made another halfhearted attempt to break free.

"I'm going to kill the assholes interrupting this." Eric pushed her hair aside and bit hard.

The pain from his sharp fangs shocked her but not more than the intense ecstasy racing through to her womb. She cried out as she came, her nerve endings spasming as a strange lethargy overtook her.

Eric held her when she sagged. "You're not escaping me again, sweet. Not now that you wear my bite. Logan, grab her something to wear."

She heard Logan sigh. Dominic muttered something about protecting the group downstairs. A flutter of reason intruded. "Sean?" she asked, but couldn't be sure they understood. Her lips felt numb, her tongue was swollen and her teeth ached, all of which scared the hell out of her.

Energy pulsed in waves around the room, letting her feel what they felt. The males sweltered with frustrated desire and sheer rage. Her own release drained her while making her itch for something more.

Someone laid her back on the bed and pushed and prodded her into a shirt, jeans and shoes. She sensed Jesse near. How she could differentiate him from the others in this state she didn't know. He didn't "resonate" as intensely as Eric or Dominic, but he felt familiar.

"We'll have to postpone this again." He gently lifted her and placed her over his shoulder, his hand firm as he stroked her ass. "Don't worry, baby. You'll be taking us soon enough."

She moaned, knowing she shouldn't want what she desperately craved.

"It's okay," Logan added. "What do you think, Dom?"

"I don't recognize them as Salinas. I'm thinking Chen's men."

"Our Vicki's a very popular woman, it seems." Eric again. He didn't sound happy. "Good thing we found you first, sweet."

Vicki wanted to protest. She wasn't sweet. She didn't want sex with Voiders. She wanted a real relationship with someone normal, or so she kept telling herself. Her vision grayed and she shook her head. Or at least, she tried to shake her head. That slight movement finally did her in. She lost control over her body and passed out cold.

"She's gone." Jesse held their prize over his shoulder.

"Let's go," Eric growled as he zipped up his pants. He didn't bother with a shirt and shifted into his *guer*, his stronger form—a massive frame, dark brown fur, fangs and claws capable of decimating his opponents.

"I've got a bag for her." Logan held up a duffel full of Vicki's things. "She has great taste in lingerie, by the way."

Dom groaned. "She has the devil's own luck. That she managed to throw us the first time still amazes me. Once again we're interrupted from taking her. Fucking Chen and his men."

As king of the Ravagers on this foreign world, Eric didn't normally wait on anyone. The situation with this female pissed him the hell off. He should have been buried to the root in her by this point. Once again he was enraged and frustrated, though he couldn't help feeling pleased about the chase. Victoria Fox turned out to be a real challenge, in more ways than one.

Dom had been right to choose her. As royal guard, he at times knew more about Eric's needs than Eric did. This female, a rare Conduit, satisfied that thirst inside him for sex and something more. Eric didn't understand his fierce fascination, but he had no intention of letting her go before he'd satisfied his curiosity. Biting her, physically marking her flesh, barely eased his crushing need to possess. No doubt sex with Vicki would be fan-fucking-tastic. He was still hard. The feel of her pussy around his cock…

"Prime, we need to go." Dom's eyes gleamed with amusement and his own frustration.

Eric bared his teeth and stormed from the room, content his pack would follow. He found Vicki's cousin at the mercy of the females. Diana licked at Sean's cock while Kate kissed him, adding to the sexual energy dicking with his head.

Morely groaned, arching into their handling.

"Company's coming. Get to safety," he growled at his packmates. When neither female answered, he nodded at Logan.

"Come on, ladies. You can fuck him later, Diana." Logan gave Kate an odd look, one he shared with Jesse. "I don't think he's expecting company, are you, Morely?"

"Oh God. You can't stop. Not now," he rasped, and Eric understood his pain. "What company?"

"Take Vicki to the compound," Eric ordered Jesse, tossing him Vicki's car keys he'd earlier appropriated. "Dom, let's take care of this Chen problem. Logan, join us once you've helped the females get it together." He snarled at his sex-drunk packmates. Trust Diana and Kate to add to his frustration. Watching them play with Sean reminded him of what Vicki could have been doing to *him*.

The Void love them, but his extended family aggravated the hell out of him. Normal packs consisted of a lead female and her male providers. Somehow, he'd gotten stuck with Kate and Diana, two orphaned Ravagers he'd rescued years ago. They refused to mate, refused to leave his pack and did nothing at all sexually for him or the males in his family. Though an odd circumstance, he'd seen it as his duty to provide for them. Ravagers were brutal by nature, but they respected their females with the utmost loyalty.

Which meant he couldn't leave their new plaything at home. Now, it seemed, he'd have to make room for yet *another* Conduit. As if Vicki weren't enough.

Logan helped Diana and Kate regain their bearings. Eric left the house with Dom and they hid in the alleyway from which the stench of threat emanated. A dozen men armed with guns and knives approached. The scent of gun oil burned Eric's nose. He nodded to Dom.

As one, they effectively took out the leaders, using them as shields when the others shot at them. Four men fell while the others took cover behind whatever they could find. Dom and Eric sprang apart. Eric used an ancient truck to shield him from a spray of bullets while Dom swiftly shifted and took out two of the enemy.

Logan appeared behind the group and worked on them from that angle. When changed, he and Jesse could pass as twins. Their scents were the same, save for a subtle difference only Kate seemed able to identify.

The minute the bullets stopped, Eric leapt from his position and crashed into a group aiming knives at Dom. The four remaining enemy had been reduced to moaning on the cold, hard ground. Injured but alive. Eric wanted answers.

"Why are you here?" he asked through sharp teeth.

Two humans stared up at him in shock, while the Voiders tried to avoid his glare. They at least knew not to look directly at a Ravager in a rage.

Obviously caught in battle lust and unable to stop himself, Dom tore out the throats of the humans. "Never challenge the prime," he snarled.

Eric detected the scent of fear on the unknown Voider closest to him. The scent fed his appetite for destruction. These bastards had been after Vicki, after what he now considered *his*.

"Speak," he ordered in a low voice.

The calm Voider, a Valk, shifted into a sitting position. He had pointed ears, pale skin and the ability to shatter glass with his voice, yet he spoke in a rough tone. "I have information you might want." He'd obviously sustained vocal cord damage at some point in his life, explaining his sudden capitulation when faced with Ravagers. Valks were known to be vicious, and Eric was disappointed he wouldn't get the fight he wanted from this one.

"Don't keep the prime waiting." Dom lifted the Valk to his feet and shook him by the scruff of the neck. Dom's long claws inflicted damage on the male's white skin.

Logan licked his lips when the scent of blood filled the air.

"Tommy Chen wants his ring back. Your, ah, the woman, Victoria Fox, stole it. It's Chen's rightful property. He doesn't want a turf war; he just wants his ring."

"And the woman," the nervous Voider still on the ground added, his voice tremulous. "Has to make an example—"

"Shut up, Haverson." The Valk who Dom held kicked Haverson in the face with a speed Eric could respect. "Our orders were to find the ring. Chen wants to take care of the woman personally."

Dom grunted and dropped him to the ground.

"What's your name?" Eric asked.

The Valk swallowed hard. "Walker."

"Well, then, Walker. Today's your lucky day." Eric broke Walker's wrist with a snap. He hissed in pain but made no loud noises. Haverson didn't fare so well. At a nod from Eric, Dom broke his neck. "You're going to keep tabs on Chen for me. You know your way around Ravagers and apparently Chen. Go back with a sign that you at least put up a fight," he paused to nod at the Valk's wrist, "and he'll let you live. He'll bloody you, but once you heal, you can be my eyes and ears."

"If I say no?" Walker wisely refused to look at him. His quiet defiance soothed Eric's need to punish. Eric respected intelligence and grit, and Walker appeared to have both.

"Then I'll kill you, clean." Eric ran his claws across Walker's neck, leaving a line of blood that immediately healed.

"Fine." Walker sighed and relaxed, no longer insolent. "I didn't really like working for Chen anyway. But the pay's good, and it keeps the Salinas off my ass."

"Go to a Ravager bar called The Cave tomorrow and leave your number. Don't fuck with me, or you'll wish for death by the time I'm through with you."

"I get it, I swear." He glanced at Dom then looked away again. "Savage Clan, right?"

Dom grinned and stepped between Eric and Walker. "Yeah."

"One other thing you might want to know." Walker inched back, keeping his gaze averted. "The Lawlesses have been sniffing around Chen, trying to make a deal. Just something to keep in mind."

Dom grunted. "Take off."

Walker disappeared without sound, running down the alley the way he'd come.

"That sucked." Logan shook his head and morphed back into his more human frame. "Not enough time to really get into a good lather."

Eric and then Dom resumed their other forms as well.

"We were ready to get into 'a good lather' before we were interrupted," Dom reminded him. "I'm still hungry. Let's head back to the homestead and get the pussy that got away."

Eric chuckled. "I hate cats. But for Vicki, I'll make an exception."

Logan and Dom joined him in the vehicle. Kate and Diana had already driven off with Sean—the other non-Ravager Eric would be forced to deal with. He sighed.

"What do you think?" Eric asked Dom from the backseat of their SUV as Logan drove.

In tune with one another, Dom didn't have to ask what he meant. "I think the female's going to lead you on one helluva chase. And let's face it. You need the challenge. What's the last thing you've hunted that got away?"

"Vicki," Logan answered with a snicker.

The damn pup.

Dom smacked him in the back of the head.

"What?" Logan was still grinning.

"Watch your tone." Dom sighed. "You're the least disciplined of the pack, yet we keep you. Why is that, Prime?"

Eric chuckled. "Because he's good with his mouth?" Dom flushed, and Eric laughed louder. "Why is my guard so shy when it comes to sex? You're turning human on us, Dom."

"Not one word," Dom warned Logan when he opened his mouth.

Wisely, the Ravager closed it.

"I can't remember the last time we fucked a decent female," Eric grumbled. "The humans around here aren't enough." Playing devil's advocate, he sought his pack's opinion. "Maybe Jesse has the right of it. We should make peace with the Lawless clan and look for a mate there."

The horror on Logan's and Dom's faces reinforced his original decision. "Relax. I was just thinking out loud. Obviously, you're on the same page I am. None of the Lawless clan are to be trusted, leaving the future of our clan to non-Ravager Voiders."

"And Conduits," Logan offered. "Vicki smells right."

"Yeah." Dom exhaled heavily. "Everything about her vibrates on your level," he said to Eric. "Physically, mentally…even her *guer*, as untrained as it is, suits you."

A Ravager's *guer*, his fighting spirit, was all to their kind. The wilder the *guer*, the stronger the Ravager. Animal instincts went hand in hand with resilience. Coming from a world where only the fittest survived, Ravagers only chose the best to carry on their lines.

With a slim ratio of female to male Ravagers, they'd had to make a decision. The king before Eric, like all the rest, had refused to allow Ravagers to procreate with others outside their kind. The stress of life in this world, and his cruelty, turned his into a short-lived reign and fractured the Ravagers into two clans. One followed Eric, the Savages, and the other followed Nev Lawless, the Lawless clan.

Nev was a sick bastard, one who reveled in brutality over his Ravagers and the humans unfortunate enough to come into contact with him. The Salinas couldn't contain him, but Eric and his warriors did. Though mostly banished to the fields skirting the Boundary, and smaller in number than the Savages, the Lawless clan posed a constant threat. If he could have, Eric would have killed every damn one of them. But he couldn't rule his kind and push for their future while engaging in a race war. His Ravagers needed the promise of family, of tomorrow, not more death over territory disputes and the validity of Ravager mating practices.

"Prime?" Dom frowned.

Did he really want to think about Nev Lawless when he had a nearly marked female waiting at home for him? "Drive faster, Logan. I'm hungry."

Logan nodded. "Can't argue with that. Don't hit me again, Dom." He shot Dom a dark look. "It's a figure of speech.

I wouldn't really argue with Prime. Hell, I'm having a hard time thinking about anything besides sinking into Vicki. This is the first time Prime's ever marked a female. I didn't think it would be so... The need has never been this intense before." He sounded confused.

Join the club.

"So how long are you going to keep her, anyway?"

Eric started. He didn't know. It wasn't as if he could take her to mate, to claim her. Sex was one thing, but a permanent joining? And why was he even thinking about forever with a virtual stranger?

Dom licked his lips. "I'm thinking Prime is going to need some time to break this one in."

Vicki wouldn't give in easily. He knew she wouldn't. It wasn't in her nature, just as he knew sex with her would be incredible.

"She'll need a firm hand, Prime. Guidance. Others to show her what you like, what you need."

"Dammit, Dom." Logan shifted in his seat. "I'm trying to drive and this hard-on isn't helping."

"No shit." Eric glared. "Shut up already, or consider yourself last in tonight's lineup."

Dom turned to stare at Eric in surprise. He met Eric's displeasure for several heartbeats before he slowly looked away. "Touchy bastard," he muttered.

"What's that?" Eric forced himself not to smile. Trust Dom never to give an inch.

"Sorry." He sounded as if he wanted to shove that sorry down Eric's throat, and Eric knew, had Logan not been present, he probably would have tried.

Logan coughed but didn't quite hide his laughter. When Dom snarled, Logan quickly changed the subject to Kate and Diana. While he and Dom discussed Sean Morely and what the girls might really want with him, Eric envisioned Vicki and the brewing battle he'd have winning her over.

How long would he keep her? His *guer* didn't like the question. *As long as I need to,* he told himself. *Or longer.*

Chapter Four

Vicki's head pounded, waking her from a deep rest. Memories of Ravagers and her cousin returned, and she wondered what mess she'd landed in now. The last thing she recalled, Jesse had tossed her over his shoulder.

"So why am I in a bed? And where is this place?" After sitting up, she edged off the gigantic bed and stumbled to the window to gather her bearings. She took a deep, cleansing breath and looked out at a forest under the breaking dawn. No Salinas, no criminals or crowded streets. Jesse must have taken her somewhere outside the city limits, because the picturesque background outside seemed far from the overcrowded city that was Cross Step.

A perimeter of green grass surrounded the house, some of it covered in orange and red leaves that tumbled from the massive trees in the wood line. Beyond the grass she saw a blanket of forest. From out of the woods, several Ravagers appeared in their beastlike forms. Most likely she stood inside their headquarters, a safehouse, or something like it. She'd have a devil of a time escaping, even if she did manage her way out of this house unmolested.

As her mind whirred with options, she investigated and found a bathroom. Making good use of it, she felt like herself once more and left the bathroom with purpose—to ignore the pulsing, sexual need thrumming through her body, find and rescue her cousin and get the hell out of Dodge.

Before she could accomplish any one of those, the door to the bedroom opened, revealing a tall, dark stranger. Oddly enough, he vibrated with the same intense power Eric and Dom did. His sexual energy revved her own.

Not good.

"Ah. No wonder they wanted you closeted in here." The guy smiled, and she wasn't surprised to see sharp white teeth in that handsome face. "I'm Malcolm. Do you need anything, Ms. Fox?"

"Actually, I do." Vicki lunged at him and hugged him tight. As she did, she inhaled his energy, filling the reserve she'd tapped before she'd blacked out. Drawing more than she needed, she put Malcolm on his ass. He dropped into a heap, and she winced when his head struck the wooden floor.

"Sorry," she whispered. Skirting around him, she cautiously left the bedroom and shut the door behind her. She closed her eyes, let out a tendril of energy, and encountered more bodies in the house.

Opening her eyes, she turned right and ran down the hallway, down a flight of stairs and out a side door. She thought it odd that no one tried to stop her. Though she hadn't seen anyone this way, surely someone kept watch on all corners of the house. But not wanting to question her luck, she tore across the grass into the woods.

Wishing she knew where the hell she was going, Vicki nonetheless ran as if her life depended on it. Catching her breath when she'd run a reasonable distance, she leaned against a tree, pleased to have expended some energy with her escape. In her haste to get away, she'd drawn too much from Malcolm. A stupid mistake she shouldn't have made. Now she had to reconcile a balance.

She wondered what Eric and the others would do when they found her missing. Rubbing the aching mark on her neck, she stubbornly ignored the corresponding flare of heat in her sex. Damn Ravager bite.

"Have a nice run?" The low voice froze her to the spot.

Slowly straightening, she glanced to her left. Logan and Jesse stood with their arms crossed over their chests...their *naked* chests.

Immediately turning in the opposite direction, she checked herself from taking a step. Eric and Dominic grinned at her. Sheer hunger shone in their eyes and their bodies, their cocks standing stiffly at attention.

"Such lovely prey," Eric murmured, fixated on her mouth.

"I'm nobody's prey," she spat, adrenaline coursing through her. She had to be a nut to be turned-on by four aroused Ravagers. Hell, the last time they'd been together, Eric had bitten her.

Vicki took a step back and stopped. Jesse and Logan stood right behind her. She had to deal with those two. Unfortunately, her run had drained enough energy that she needed to recharge before taking on the four of them.

Eric fisted his erection, holding out his excitement like an offering. His blue eyes blazed like neon lights in the shaded daylight. Streams of sunlight glistened over his skin like water, a smooth glow highlighting every muscle and bulge on the man.

Vicki swallowed audibly.

"Come here." Eric crooked a finger at her, and she scowled.

"Hell, no."

"God, I love it when they fight," Dominic said on a groan as he rubbed his shaft.

"Stop it right now. Put your clothes back on. I mean it," she said to Eric and backed up another step. She couldn't help it. When he moved closer, she retreated, an instinctive need for flight.

"I'm going to bend you over and fuck you," Eric rasped. "My dick is hard, so tight with the need to come. Let's feel that pussy again, hmm, pet?"

"I'll give you 'pet'," she muttered and sprung at him. Vicki gripped Eric's forearms and tried to siphon his energy. Unlike the last time, he didn't release it, but used their tie to bring *her* closer to *him*. She quickly let him go. "What did you do?" she whispered, stunned that he manipulated her so easily, especially since she'd been on her guard.

"You surprised me once. But fool me twice, shame on me. I shifted my *guer*. You might find it harder to control me now." He grinned, showing a lot of teeth. "Closer, sweet. You have too many clothes on." He nodded to the men behind her.

She did her best, but after a few minutes she wore nothing but the skin God gave her.

The men surrounding her exuded power, lust and need like a living, breathing entity.

Vicki tried to take a step back and Eric pounced.

The feel of his skin against hers stunned her. Like a static blanket of electricity, her body hummed and sighed, fitting against his perfectly.

She wanted to fight and struggled, if only to make him tighten his grip.

"That's it," he said thickly. "Squirm. Fight it, sweet."

"You can't just have me," she said, a weak defense. *But he's had me since I first touched those firm lips of his.*

"But I can."

"And he will," Dominic added. "The prime takes what he wants when he wants."

"His will, his way," Logan said from directly behind her.

"Hold her," Eric commanded the others. Jesse held her arms behind her back while Dominic and Logan spread her thighs wide. To her alarm, they gripped her ankles. Vicki couldn't move.

"You can't—" She sucked in a breath as Eric dropped to his knees and spread her folds with his fingers. Without pause, he set his lips over her clit and sucked. "*Eric.*"

"Take her foot," Dominic said. In seconds, he'd let go of her and someone else latched on to her ankle. Dom circled around her and fastened his lips to her breast, licking and biting with a roughness that did more than arouse her. Then Eric shocked her by shoving a finger inside her.

That quickly, her orgasm burst over her.

She cried out and jolted, startled anew when Eric sank his teeth into her sensitive inner thigh. His bite didn't last long. In seconds, he let her go and tore her from the others. Carrying through on his threat, he bent her over a broken tree covered with moss. Eric pushed her belly-down and nudged her thighs apart. On the other side of the tree Dominic grabbed her hands and held her taut, so she couldn't move.

"Eric, Dominic, let me go," Vicki breathed, still tense from her orgasm as well as excited by their domination.

"She creamed. I can smell it," Jesse said. "She's creaming even more. That's good, Vicki."

As if she was trying to be excited. She couldn't help it if her body wanted the attention.

"You're mine now, Vicki," Eric said as he mounted her. "Tell me you don't want this and I'll let you go."

She quivered, unable to help herself, at the feel of his chest against her back, his thighs brushing the backs of her legs. Never in her life had she been so incredibly turned-on. Eric was all around her, his scent, his touch. And the others watched. She could sense their need, could feel their eyes on her like a physical caress. She wanted to say no. The common sense inside her shrieked at her to say it. "God, I want you *so much*."

His cock pushed at her wet entrance then slammed home.

Startled at the violence of the action, she cried out. Eric was fucking her, thrusting hard with speed and force. And he felt so incredibly good.

"More," she heard herself demand, as if someone else.

"Oh yeah," Dom encouraged. "Ride her."

Vicki could only groan, taking Eric's passion as he grunted and surged. He fucked her forever, reaching around her body and between her thighs to tease her clit as he took her until she came again.

When she cried out, he clutched her hips and shuddered on a low, hoarse groan.

He remained locked inside her as he bent down to cover the mark on her neck with his teeth. Euphoria filled her, a sense of belonging to this powerful male who overwhelmed her. Her arms dangled over the log and she belatedly realized Dominic had let her go when Eric stepped away. Then another male fucked her. Harder pounding almost as intense and just as thrilling as Eric's taking. Right before he finished, he pulled out and came all over her back. He bit her, covering Eric's bite with his own.

"Ours," Dominic growled, his voice decidedly feral. He licked her shoulder to stem the flow of blood, then turned her head and kissed her. A wave of energy filled her before he stepped away from her.

She immediately regretted his loss, her body like a foreign thing that wanted nothing but pleasure.

"Now it's our turn to cement Prime's mark," Logan decreed and pulled Vicki off the tree like a rag doll.

"Oh," she gasped, trying to catch her breath. Dominic's encounter had recharged her engine, and she wanted to climax again.

Logan set Vicki down on a bed of grass on her knees. "Now we're going to finish tying you to Prime. Swallow us," he demanded, positioning his cock at her mouth.

Jesse stood next to him. She could feel his excitement calling to her, pulling her back into the carnality of the moment. He held himself, waiting.

Never in her wildest dreams would Vicki have imagined sex with four men, let alone blowing two men at the same time. But the sheer energy seething around her called like to like. She needed to take what they offered, needed to give back the ecstasy she'd just experienced, if only to sate the greedy woman begging to belong.

As she knelt before them, she took Logan between her lips and sucked. First on the head, then further down his shaft, licking and stroking with a tongue that wanted more. While she played with him, she fisted her hand around Jesse, learning his size through touch.

He groaned and pushed, fucking her hand while Logan petted her hair, encouraging her to take more of him in her mouth.

Never one to engage in oral unless fully committed to a relationship, she didn't have much experience giving head. So when Logan pushed harder, she choked and backed away.

Then Eric was there. He pushed her on to her hands and knees and thrust hard, filling her with himself again. "Feed off my power. Let it take you where you need to be."

His words didn't make sense until she allowed herself to accept Eric's energy. In seconds, the rapacious hunger he felt surged inside her. She opened her mouth on a moan and swallowed Logan's shaft, deep to the back of her throat.

The gag reflex she expected didn't happen, and she sighed around Logan as he fucked her mouth with heavy moans. He pulled out and she gave Jesse equal attention. Though not as thick, he was longer than Logan but more gentle. He slowly moved in and out of her mouth, the taste of his pre-cum surprisingly sweet.

As she licked and sucked Eric's packmates, she played with their balls, their thighs, anything and everything she could reach to better hold on to her partners. The furious desire built again, as if she hadn't just come and come hard.

She groaned as Eric increased his pace, hitting that sensitive spot inside her. Fully engaged in Jesse one minute and Logan the next, she could do little more than rise to bliss as Eric pounded inside her, racing to climax.

As they approached ecstasy, she felt something warm spatter on her back and realized Dom had come again. He rubbed it into her skin just as Logan came hard down her throat. Like Jesse, he tasted sugary, a drugging cream that acted like an aphrodisiac, addicting her to swallow more.

Not content to wait any longer, Jesse pushed her hand from his cock, pulled Logan away and then thrust between her lips. He came in an instant.

Hands pulled at her nipples and clit, stimulating her from every angle. Dominic and Logan had come but weren't finished with her yet.

"Fuck, I'm coming hard," Eric roared, shooting deep.

Helpless to do anything less than accept him, she continued to swallow Jesse as she came, the pinch on her clit too much.

"Rub it in, Dom," Eric growled, withdrew and milked his cock over her back, right where Dom had spent. "Seal us together."

Jesse pulled out and leaned down, placing a hard, wet kiss over the mark on her neck. Logan did the same. Eric helped her to her feet and bit her hard again, right over that same damn spot.

But instead of heat, she felt a deep, numbing cold, one that consumed her like a frost, holding her still. Pinpricks of desire, pain, and then a sudden firestorm caused her to cry out as she swayed.

Eric caught her while the others steadied her, stroking her heated skin as if petting a wild animal. With tender, slow strokes.

When her mind cleared of the chaos flooding her from head to toe, she stood and blinked into Eric's ice-blue eyes.

"Now, Vicki, you belong to me. You're pack." Eric looked entirely too pleased with himself. He kissed her hard and slapped her on the ass.

"That was just the beginning," Dominic said from behind her. He shoved into her lower back with an impossible-to-miss erection. "Wait 'til you see what we can do with a bed."

* * * * *

After dressing in the rags they'd left of her clothes, Vicki followed the men at a much more leisurely pace and wondered what the hell to think. Four men. Not one. Not even two. But *four* insatiable Ravagers. Holy shit, talk about a secret she'd take to her grave.

Yet she'd had the best sexual experience of her life. What did that say about her? *That I'm a pervert maybe? Or a slut? Maybe an orgy gal, one ready to make my big break into the lucrative field of PAN, the Porn-All the time-Network.*

She tried thinking of a new name to call herself but could come up with nothing better than Vicki the Voider Lover. Lame, and much too tame for these animals. Literally.

Who the hell would have guessed they'd give her such intense ecstasy? No wonder more and more people turned to Voiders for kicks. But was the intensity of loving so great because she'd been marked, or was it the men themselves?

And how do I look at myself in the mirror having been with four freakin' guys at the same time? As great as it was, I don't think I can do that again. Not without walking bowlegged for the rest of my life.

"You all right, Vicki?" Jesse asked, smirking at her ripped clothing. "Better than that shirt, at least."

"I don't know," Logan teased and grazed her exposed nipple with a finger. "I think the rips add a certain charm."

"A slutty charm, maybe."

When Logan wiggled his eyebrows at her, she muttered, "Ass," and tried not to smile. Try as she might, she couldn't be angry with them, and that baffled her. She should have been enraged. They'd practically raped her in the woods. *Oh really? Is that why when Eric gave you a chance to stop it, you begged him to finish?* She flushed and hurried to Eric. She had to grab him by the wrist and yank to stop him, which halted everyone else as well. They really were a pack, she reminded herself.

"Yes?" His eyes gleamed with warmth as he stared at her.

She wanted to demand that the fivesome—*God help me, a fivesome*—never happen again. But she couldn't deny she'd enjoyed it. "Explain the bite marks," she said instead. She swallowed hard. "The marking. My cousin said it makes you crazy for Ravager sex. Is that true?"

Eric and the others exchanged a glance. "Not necessarily. The mark makes it easier for me to find you. It adds my scent to yours so that any other Ravagers will steer clear, knowing where you belong."

"Like a possession?" she asked, ice coating her words.

"Exactly. I own you, now. Accept it."

She met him stare for stare. "*You* own *me*? Because this says otherwise," she teased as she grazed his hardened cock with her fingers. Pleased she wasn't the only one with an addiction, she let him go when his gaze narrowed and his breath grew shallow. "Looks to me like I own *you*, Prime." She snorted with amusement, turned her back on him and walked away.

She heard a scuffle and over her shoulder saw Dom holding him back. Not a smart move to show her back to the enemy, but this particular enemy seemed to thrive on challenge. Eric and the others had mentioned more than once how much they prized a fight. They were in for the fight of their lives if they thought she'd roll over and beg any time soon.

Logan caught up to her. "Nice one."

"Yeah," Jesse said from her other side. He wore a grin, the first she'd seen on his somber face. "I think Dom was right about you."

"Right about what?"

"Well, Dom knows things. He's Eric's guard. And the prime's guard is totally in tune with the prime."

"On a psychic level," Logan explained.

"Right." Jesse nodded. "Dom knows what Eric wants almost before he wants it. And Eric wants you."

"As we can tell." Logan snickered. "Man, it's been a long time since any woman's put him in his place."

"Logan," Jesse warned.

"I mean, Diana and Kate said no to him. But they're packmates, not lovers. It'll be interesting to see if your cousin can wrap Diana around his finger. Because you've already wrapped Prime around—"

His words were cut off when Eric pulled him away and shoved a fist into his gut.

Startled, Vicki automatically moved to intercede when Jesse caught her. "No. This is for Prime to handle. Logan talks too much."

Logan clutched his belly and coughed. He glanced up before bowing his head low before Eric. Then he muttered something Vicki couldn't hear. Apparently assuaged, Eric nodded and let him stand.

Eric strode to her and stopped. Vicki held her breath, waiting to see what he'd do to her. He did nothing, simply stared. The fire in his eyes reminded her of his energy, bright and so blindingly beautiful. She wanted to kiss him all over again, to bend over and let herself be taken. Aggravated with her stupid sex drive, she forgot caution and poked him in the chest.

"What the hell was that—"

Eric stopped her words with a kiss that nearly had her climaxing. When he let her go a minute later, she stumbled. He grinned. "Welcome to the family, pet."

At the sheer outrage emanating from Vicki, Eric wanted to laugh. Damn, she was hot. He wanted to fuck her again right now. Logan and his big mouth didn't know the half of it.

Coming inside her had been unlike anything he'd ever experienced. Oblivious to everything but Vicki, the feel, taste and scent of her, Eric had come hard.

She'd had no qualms telling him she didn't like feeling subservient. For an instant, she'd gotten under his skin. As if a mere female, a human at that, could bring the Ravager prime to his knees. Yet he knew the woman had power, more than those odd fluctuations of energy. Already he loathed parting from her.

He'd nearly torn Jesse a new one for leaving her alone in the house, even for a few minutes. It figured Malcolm had found her. Dom had put Malcolm in charge of security at the house, and the younger Ravager took his responsibilities seriously. New to the clan, Malcolm had been lucky enough to enter this world through a Void just two years ago. In the time since, he'd made a name for himself as a male few could resist.

Fortunately for Malcolm, Vicki had resisted. She hadn't given him a chance to take what he would have wanted. No, his little Conduit manipulated Malcolm and gave them a stimulating chase.

Having caught her and had her, Eric might have thought she'd accept she couldn't overpower them.

"You think calling me a slave is funny?" she demanded, fisting her hands on her hips. The fragrance of her anger mingled with the cream flowing between her thighs. He scented himself all over her and wanted to howl with delight. She wore his mark.

"Not funny. Sexy."

She must have seen the sexual threat in his eyes because she took a few steps back before remembering to scowl at him. "We're going to have to get a few things straight, buddy. Because taking someone's table in a bar doesn't amount to any…ownership."

"Let's save the argument for home," Dom interrupted. "Unless you'd rather get fucked again out here?"

Trust Dom to put it bluntly. He and the others were hard as stone.

Vicki flushed. She crossed her arms, plumping her breasts beneath her half-torn shirt.

Eric had allowed her to dress because it made her feel better, and it somewhat shielded her from his carnal needs. Watching her tits bounce and her ass shake as they walked home would have seen Vicki fucked until she couldn't walk. He didn't want to introduce her to the clan unable to stand on her own two feet.

"I didn't think so." Dom took her by the arm and forced her to walk.

Logan and Jesse transformed into their full *guer* and took off ahead of them. Ravagers he'd taken in as pups, he called them pack, but he hadn't claimed them. Only Dom held such a deep place in his heart and in his *guer*. The others in his pack belonged, but he couldn't shake the feeling that Logan and Jesse weren't meant to stay his forever. And the Void love them, Diana and Kate would one day claim their own males and start their own packs.

"Why did they do that?" Vicki asked in a low voice, glancing after Logan and Jesse.

"Does it bother you?" Eric asked, curious.

"What?"

"Our *guer*, our fighting spirit that others can see?"

"You mean your wolfman form? No. I've dealt with a lot of Voiders in my life, and in my opinion, you guys are good."

"Good?"

"You're the most honest. You wear yourselves plainly on the outside. Basic animal needs, you like to fight and you like to fuck. Am I missing anything?"

"No." Yet she dismissed the Ravagers as no more than beasts, and that irritated him. "But we're a thinking race as well. Not everything is dictated by lust."

"Really?" She gave him a wry look. Even Dom quirked a brow.

"It's true." Eric glared. "I can get a woman to spread her legs with the snap of a finger." Ah, his Conduit didn't like that. The annoyance on her face eased his tension. "But I don't want just anyone. I want you."

"Yeah, well..." She blushed and tried to tug free from Dom's side. "The sex was great, I'll grant you. But I'll tell you plain out that I can't do that every time you guys get an itch. The four of you will wear me out before next week."

She sounded confident that her exhaustion would recuse her from more attention.

"That's good to know. Because you're mine, Vicki. You'll only need to spread those luscious thighs for me and Dom."

"So the orgy was a onetime deal?"

"For marking, and on special occasions when my packmates warrant a treat. But your main job is to serve me."

She visibly bristled. "Dream on, wolfie. We can argue that later," she hurried to add when Dom tried to intervene. "Because I'm still not sure what the whole marking thing means, and you haven't explained it to my satisfaction. Tell me, *Prime*, why the hell did you really bite me?" Her gaze narrowed. "Are you working for Chen?"

Dom snorted. "Chen should be so lucky. Prime leads the Ravagers on this planet." At her blank look, he explained. "He's our king, Vicki. No less than the leader of the Ravagers has chosen you as royal consort. He can keep you as long as he wants, for whatever purpose he wants."

Vicki opened her mouth then snapped it closed. The fight in her eyes hadn't extinguished, and the *guer* inside Eric purred with satisfaction.

"That's right, sweet. You're mine until I say otherwise." *And I'm not even close to being done with you. Not now, maybe not ever.*

Chapter Five

"The Savage prime's taken a human." The Lawless cur spoke in a low voice, his head bowed, his entire mien a study in submission. Nev Lawless grunted his dismissal, pleased when the Ravager left without another word.

Will, his personal guard and second-in-command, shook his head. "What the hell is Eric thinking? A human?" He sneered and chanced a look at Nev. "Do we kill her or take her?"

"We can't play with her if she's dead. Take her, I think." Nev and Will shared a smile. Then, scenting prey in the wind, Nev carefully crept from his place on the rock he liked to think of as his throne. Keeping to tradition, he remained in his natural form—his *guer*; his enhanced senses made the world crisper. Colors were brighter, smells riper. In the earthy forests and fields on the outskirts of town that bordered the government's no-pass zone, *real* Ravagers roamed the night.

Glad to be himself, even in this hellish place, Nev found what he'd been after. Moments later, a fat, juicy rabbit dangled from his bloodied claws. It squirmed to be free, finally slowing its movements until the spark of life left its bleak brown eyes. The fresh meat sated his appetite, at least for food. His belly full for the next hour, he turned to the other pressing need making it uncomfortable to walk.

Returning to the cave, he called home, he sought Will, who busily rutted between a sobbing human's thighs. Watching his packmate take the female, Nev couldn't help wondering what Will thought as he fucked her. Ever since Diana and Kate Savage had rejected him, Will had become more cruel than ever. A fitting temperament for the guard of the next *true* Ravager king.

"Should I make the kidnapping public or a secret?" Will rasped as he finished spending in the woman. He pulled out and pushed her aside.

She stumbled and fell next to her blubbering friend, another attractive human with light-colored hair, large breasts and ample hips. Sturdy, hard to break and fun to "ravage".

"So eager, aren't you, Will?" Nev licked his lips, intrigued with the coppery liquid clinging to the brunette's thighs, like the blood that lingered on his lips from his recent kill. "We'll wait a bit, keep an eye on the Savages and make sure Eric's new toy is important enough to rate his worry. Who knows? He may just be amusing himself with a human."

"A Conduit," Will corrected and snarled at the blonde trying to crawl away. He slapped a chain from the cave wall to the collar around her neck and locked her down. The moon hid behind a cloud, and darkness settled over them. In the brief moment of silence, Will's breathing and the females' cries for mercy echoed within the cave.

Outside, the rest of the Lawless clan played with whatever they felt like. Unlike Eric and his idiotic notions of change, Nev preferred the old ways. Might made right. Out here, Ravagers ruled the land. Any human or Voider stupid enough to trespass on Lawless territory deserved a slow, painful death.

"A Conduit," he repeated to Will with vague understanding, his concentration on the growing hunger between his legs.

"A human with gifts. Psychic abilities that resonate with Void energy," Will explained, as he had countless times before.

"Norm. Conduit. They still stink of human, inferior to clan."

"For certain." Will showed his teeth to the human, who unfortunately saw nothing in the dark. Weak, like the rest of her kind.

Nev respected strength. Other Voiders he might not like, but he appreciated their power. The Valk could pierce eardrums with their screeching voices. Lites blended into any environment and became invisible. Vulcani harnessed alien fire. And Tommy Chen, the things that "man" could do...

A dozen or more species of Voiders lived in Cross Step alongside the Ravagers. All of them had more of his esteem than the pathetic natives of this world. He still had a hard time believing Voiders and the feeble humans of Earth had any relationship whatsoever. Yet, he couldn't deny their compatible physiologies.

With a sigh, he recognized his pressing needs for the human treat just a few yards away. He felt Will's interest and allowed his guard to watch.

It didn't take Nev long. His first and second climaxes came all too quickly. But he took his time achieving the next two. To his surprise, the blonde remained alive and aware throughout his taking.

A glimpse of her pale hair made him think of another blond, one he'd coveted for many years—Dominic, Eric's guard, the man who'd once belonged to Nev, his servant and best friend in another life, in another place.

Glaring at the reminder of Dom—yet another loss at Eric Savage's hands—Nev withdrew from the sniveling woman and gave her to Will, who rode her hard.

Predictably, she expired.

"Not bad. She lasted longer than I'd thought she would." Will grinned, his teeth flashing in the darkness as he pushed her away. Muffled whimpering drew his attention, and he took care of the brunette as well. One swift bite to the throat and the sweet smell of blood layered over the sex already lingering in the dank cave.

"Dump the bodies," Nev growled, still hungry for something he couldn't quite name.

Will nodded, unchained the women and dragged them from the cave. He laughed at something someone outside said.

The minute he disappeared from view, Nev felt his absence. The curse of Ravager existence, that pack-like mentality. It had never bothered him at home, where everyone was the same. But here, among so many other races, he saw frailties in his kind he was determined to eradicate.

Annoyed that the aloneness smothered him, Nev forced himself to be strong and paced to push away the vulnerability a leader couldn't afford to feel. But without the presence of others to distract him from the past, memories invaded, the way they always did, pulling at the dark silence inside him, reminding him of the weakness that ran in his blood.

As if he'd passed through only yesterday, Nev recalled the coldness leeching into his bones, the shrieking things clawing at his *guer* and ripping at his sanity as he screamed his way through an intradimensional portal to this place — through *the Void*. He suppressed a shudder, wondering why his father hadn't met the threat invading their world head-on.

The once-great leader of the Ravagers had chosen to deny his duty. He'd ignored the needs of his clan and shoved his family through the Void before destroying the cave in which it sat, effectively killing more than half his brethren in the process, Nev had later heard. If not for the sister Void on their nearby moon, which allowed so many others to escape, he never would have known the fate of his family. And never would have had to deal with Eric Savage and his brood either, he thought with disgust.

The Dekken would have annihilated the homeworld by now. The new Ravagers setting foot in Cross Step came from surrounding worlds, where they'd made hasty escapes. Of the millions of Ravagers who managed to evade the Dekken, hardly any found their way to Earth. If only they could figure out how the fucking Voids worked.

Nev wished he'd journeyed to another world, where his kind might have taken charge and established a commanding order. The thought of Cross Step being the last home to so few Ravagers made him want to kill all the weak humans currently running the planet into the ground. What made it so much worse was that Eric Savage and his fucked-up clan tainted their future by allowing so much impure crossbreeding.

Nev ignored the regret welling within and resolved to bring the clans together again. If not for Eric Savage, the Ravagers might have been strong enough to take over this pathetic city. It wasn't as if they had anywhere else to go. Passing back through the Voids wouldn't guarantee safety on arrival at the other end, wherever the hell that might be. And the United States government had an impenetrable boundary around the forty square miles of what they called "Cross Step, The Restricted Area".

Instead of making the best of it, Eric chose to live in peace among non-Ravagers. He had the nerve to put aside his own history by allowing his Ravagers to mate with those outside their own kind, a source of constant strife at home.

Ravagers needed sex the way they needed to feed. A rapacious hunger filled the species, which was probably why nature had made so few Ravager females. With the amount of fucking they did, Ravagers would take over the universe if not held in check.

Packs of four now grew to packs of six and seven, to better the chance of new offspring. Fucking humans and other Voiders wasn't a concern. Ravagers took care of sexual desire with whomever they wanted, race and gender mattered not. But bringing mixed-blood offspring into this world screamed of heresy, an abomination the last king had tried so hard to end by disallowing permanent unions with non-Ravagers.

Eric knew this, yet he kept in his own pack two pureblood females and took neither to mate! The male was not only a fool but an illogical beast without the intelligence to lead. How he'd garnered so much support within the Ravager community remained a mystery to Nev. But no matter. Given time, Nev had every intention of taking back what was rightfully his.

He flexed his fingers and stared at his bloodstained claws. Power thrived in his *guer*, in the animal strength of primitive right. Who were the Savages to thumb their noses at tradition?

No one. They are nothing more than the crusted blood beneath my fingers. A strand of blonde hair caught in the jagged end of a nail. He stared at it and wondered if Eric's new female had such light-colored hair or if Dominic remained the token blond in the clan.

He was still holding the strand when Will reentered the cave.

* * * * *

Monday morning, after a useless day and night spent arguing to go free, or at the least, see her cousin, Vicki sat across from Eric and Dom in Eric's study. She'd had free rein of the house yesterday, but anytime she tried to leave, Ravagers blocked her. Despite the comfort of the bed they'd offered her, she'd spent the night twisting and turning, unable to sleep.

She shifted her gaze from Dominic to Eric and back again. She'd had sex not just with any Ravagers. "Prime" wasn't just the title for the head of the household but for the freakin' king.

Eric and Dom studied her, making her more than uncomfortable while she waited for someone to speak. Logan and Jesse had gone, seeing to other matters as ordered by Eric. Thankfully, yesterday Eric had given her one of his shirts to replace the one he and the others had ripped. She'd knotted it at the waist and tried to pretend she wore a bra beneath, that the thin fabric didn't highlight the peaks of her hardened nipples. Logan, the ass, had refused to give her any of her own clothes when she'd clearly seen him toting her duffel bag through the house.

She crossed her arms to hide her breasts, annoyed she remained in a constant state of arousal when around these two.

Bad enough she couldn't help her reaction to the arrogant Ravagers sitting across the table from her. At least they'd dressed before meeting her this morning. Some part of her had feared they'd show up naked again, insisting on more sex. The clothes were a nice attempt at civility she appreciated.

Annoyed the prime and his stubborn guard remained mute, she broke the silence, feeling as if she'd lost round one of a game she didn't know how to play. "So tell me what this marking means to me." She stubbornly refused to be any man's possession. No matter how that insane little part inside thrilled at the word. Freaked that she secretly liked the thought of becoming Eric and Dom's love toy—*so* not normal—she ignored her inner longings and concentrated on the matter at hand.

Namely, her life.

"You'll stay with us for a while." Eric drummed his fingers on the table, his gaze intense.

"How long is a while? I have a life to lead, you know. A business to run."

"Right." Dom nodded. He pushed a file at her. "S&V Retrievals. You have a stellar reputation, which is probably why Tommy Chen is after you."

She clenched her jaw. "Exactly. And why my being here could be very bad for you and your pack. Or clan. Whatever."

Eric grinned. She blinked, not having seen that small dimple in his left cheek before. Her heart raced. Hell, this man was lethal when *not* in Ravager form. His eyes twinkled. "You now belong to me, part of my family. We're pack but are all part of the Savage clan."

"Okay." Sean had gotten it right, for once. "So what about my cousin? You said those females were your packmates too, right?"

"Yes. They are." Eric frowned.

"Diana's marked Sean as hers," Dom answered. "Which technically makes him 'ours' as well," he said to Eric before turning to Vicki again. "Diana, and maybe Kate, seem fascinated by your cousin. So I don't see him leaving any time soon."

"You don't seem to understand that he and I have a business to run."

"Oh?" Eric's low growl should have threatened her. Instead, it made her wet.

"Look, it's not that I didn't like what we did yesterday." She flushed, trying to concede them something. "But kidnapping me and just, well, taking me away from my life, that's not legal."

"It is where we come from." Dom raised a brow, as if questioning her right to refuse them.

Damn it, Blondie's turning me on too. "Well, you're in Cross Step, now, wolf-boy. While I'm not a fan of the Salinas, even they don't allow human kidnappings."

"Wolf-boy?" Dom said as he and Eric exchanged glances. "Tell you what, *Foxy*, why don't you accept that you don't have a decision in this one and sit it out? Once Prime decides what to do with you, we'll let you know more."

"Prime, my ass." She shot to her feet and glared at both males. Angry energy swelled inside her, and she took pleasure in watching both men tense. "Yeah, you feel that, don't you?" She slammed a hand on the table and cracked the solid wood. "I'm giving you one damn hour to figure out the nicest way possible to say I'm sorry. Then I'm taking my cousin and we're getting the hell out of here."

Vicki stormed out of the study and followed the heavenly scent of vanilla toward the kitchen, a professional chef's wet dream. Once there, she ignored a wary Malcolm and focused on another Ravager standing near a bowl of batter. "You, at the griddle."

"Yeah?" The large Ravager with the raspy voice cocked an eyebrow, waiting. That he didn't project any of the hostility or aggression she'd sensed in the other males alleviated some of her tension, as did his tussled hair and sloppy dress. His wrinkled t-shirt and holed jeans didn't shout "enforcer" so much as "slacker".

"Gimme a stack." She'd save the *please* for people who deserved it. In her limited experience, Ravagers didn't rate manners.

"Better do it, Rule. Woman's got a mean right hook." Malcolm surprised her with a wink and a grin before leaving.

"Pancakes, coming up." Rule turned back to the stove, and Vicki took a deep breath, wondering how she planned to make good on her large gestures of defiance. Because if she really wanted to leave, and she did, how did she think she could power through a compound full of Ravagers, even with Sean's sorry help?

Twenty minutes later, she didn't much care. She felt too full to do more than digest her food. A glance at her companion showed him in no hurry to push away from the table.

"You don't talk much, do you?" she asked.

He grunted and shoveled another hunk of food into his mouth. A few Ravagers had come and gone through the kitchen while she'd been eating, but none stayed longer than to get a good look at her. Rule hadn't acknowledged any of them either.

A glance around her showed that the kitchen had more than enough space to feed two dozen comfortably. She and Rule sat at a smaller table in a nook overlooking the backyard—a vast field to the south of the house. The rolling splendor of Kansas hadn't changed much from the pictures her great-grandmother liked to whip out at Monday night dinners. Sprawling fields under a baby blue sky littered with cottony white clouds—

Shit. Monday dinner.

She looked around for a phone and saw nothing.

"Need something?" Rule asked in more of a growl than a human voice.

"Yeah, a phone." She dared him to deny her.

He shrugged. "No need for one out here."

"Why not? You don't have emergencies out here in the country?" They couldn't be more than an hour outside the city limits. Cross Step just wasn't that big.

"Prime can contact anyone he needs to."

"What, is he psychic?"

Rule ignored her and ate some more.

"Is he?" She genuinely wanted to know. It just figured she'd be taken in by the Voiders she knew the least about. Her parents had always cautioned her to keep a wary eye on Valks and Vulcani, both races of outsiders that could kill with little effort. The Ravagers mostly kept to themselves, or so she'd thought. They seemed to be pretty particular about whom they accepted into the fold.

Lucky her.

"No." Rule sighed and leaned back.

"No what?" she murmured, astonished that he'd polished off a dozen thick pancakes. "You eating for two?"

"No, he's not psychic. And I'm not eating for two. We have a high metabolism." He grinned, making him look almost appealing, despite his slovenly ways. Then again, she'd yet to meet an unattractive Ravager. Something about that wildness called to every woman seeking a bad boy, she supposed. *And that's the last thing I need.*

"I didn't see any other Ravagers in here eating breakfast."

He shrugged. "Guess Prime doesn't want 'em looking at you."

"So what makes you so special?"

"I'm the cook," he announced, as if that explained everything.

"Congratulations, Shaggy. I need a phone."

"Hey, you need more pancakes, a steak, chicken cordon bleu, I'm your man. Other than that, I can't help you." And with that, Rule stood and returned to the stove. She watched as he started cleaning up. Then something caught her eye.

"Hey, that's the newest range on the market. I thought those were inaccessible to Cross Step."

Rule didn't answer.

She took a harder look around the kitchen. To her astonishment, though the kitchen had high-end appliances, they were also state of the art. Two large Shurewaves, which had recently replaced the microwave, sat on either side of the main wall over wide countertops and large cabinets. Between them lay a funky copper hood above an expansive griddle and eight-range gas cooktop. The white counters looked pristine, without a stain to smudge them. On closer inspection, they were the new granite/white-steel amalgam that sold for a thousand dollars a square foot. Two walk-in refrigerators, as well as two walk-in freezers, lined the opposite wall across from the massive kitchen island complete with large stools.

"My mother would kill for this kitchen." And the underground contacts that allowed Ravagers access to equipment outside Cross Step.

Rule smiled. "It's home."

"But for all your gadgets, no televisions, computers or phones."

"Like I said, no need for 'em. This is Savage land. Our den. We keep outsiders out."

She still didn't understand, but Rule turned to the sink and ignored her.

Frustrated, she decided to go in search of Sean. Vicki stepped one foot outside the kitchen and stopped. In what looked like the size of a ballroom but functioned as a dining hall sat forty or more Ravagers eating in silence. None of them uttered a word when she entered. All eyes, however, centered on her.

She noted a few females interspersed with the majority of males. Everyone at the tables had dark hair. Here, Dominic would really stand out. Eric too, she figured, seeing so many pairs of dark eyes focused on her.

So much for stealing out of this place undetected today.

Deciding to take the initiative, she shored her determination and buried her unease at being surrounded by so many predators. "Anyone seen my cousin Sean? He looks just like me, only bigger."

Not surprised when no one answered, she swore under her breath, passed directly through the dining room and out the other door into the rest of the estate. Or should she say, mansion.

Holy hell, but the Ravagers had to have some money to live in a place this grand. It wasn't fancy, but the furnishings were quality, in decent shape and lived in. The place had an earthy feel, the decor something that might work best in a log cabin. Everywhere she turned she saw Ravagers sitting in pairs or groups. Always close enough to touch—

She quickly backed out of one open room where an orgy took place. *Good Lord.* These people had no problem sharing. Men and women, men and men. Didn't much seem to matter as long as someone had a slot B for tab A. Now more than curious about Ravager sex, she wouldn't have minded staying to watch. But she didn't want to give anyone the wrong impression. God forbid Eric find her goggling at some other Ravagers. Would he be jealous? For that matter, she'd had sex with him *and* his pack. Did Ravager packs share lovers with other Ravagers outside their pack?

Flushing at the thought and discomfited, she hastened to find her cousin. She entered a large foyer and ran up an expansive stairway that ended at a landing. Vicki continued up the right stairwell and paused when she reached the second floor.

The realization came late, but when it did, she felt like an utter idiot. She'd had the ability to find Sean since her fourth birthday. "Must be the shock of being surrounded by werewolves," she muttered, ignoring the quizzical stare of two more giants passing her on their way downstairs.

Casting her power, she sought tendrils of Sean's unique energy. Catching it, she followed the trail toward a corridor on her right. She passed several doors in a beige hallway and paused in front of the last one. She raised her hand to knock and heard the breathy moans of a woman enjoying herself.

Not wanting to wait any longer, she interrupted with a few hard bangs on the door.

To her relief, Sean answered dressed in a pair of jeans. Seeing her, he sighed.

"About time." He pulled a shirt over his head and said over his shoulder, "I'll be back later. Entertain *yourselves* for a while." He snarled and slammed the door behind him then hurried to the end of the hallway, staring at a blank wall.

"Um, Sean? There's nowhere to go." Maybe the Ravagers had exhausted him beyond thought. He wore no shoes, his hair stuck up in odd places, and he looked pale. The bite mark on his shoulder, however, looked completely healed.

She leaned closer to get a better look when he pushed against the wall. It opened to reveal a hidden set of stairs. They entered into a dimly lit passage, and the door closed quietly behind them.

"Secret passages too. This place has it all." Enthralled, despite her worries, Vicki followed her cousin down the stairs and through another passageway.

He stopped suddenly and waited. She felt his energy disperse and return to him. When he pushed on the wall, a doorway appeared. Through it, they entered an unoccupied library. Though small in comparison to the dining hall and living spaces, the library held two couches and several mahogany reading chairs. Books lined the walls from floor to ceiling. There were no windows and only one door, not counting the secret one through which they'd entered.

"Finally. A moment of peace. Diana showed me this yesterday." Sean exhaled on a breath and flopped onto a couch. He studied her with tired eyes. "You look better than I thought you would."

"You look like crap."

"Thanks. Don't hold back, Vic. Tell me what you really think."

"I really think we're in trouble. I've seen more than fifty Ravagers skulking around this place. The pack you and I stumbled into belong to their fucking Prime, and tonight's Great-Grandma Vicki's night for dinner."

Sean sat up, worry turning his gaze a dark amber. "Hell. We have to deal with Gran on top of this?"

"And no phones to speak of."

Sean groaned.

"But hey, things are looking up," she said with false cheer. "I gave Eric—their Prime—one hour to come to his senses and let us go." Vicki checked a nonexistent watch on her wrist. "So hey, we're almost saved."

She sagged onto the couch next to Sean and laid her head on his shoulder.

He hugged her tight, his arm around her, and kissed her forehead. "Don't worry, Vicki. I'll find a way out of this mess for us. But *you're* dealing with Gran."

"Not fair."

"Better you than me. Besides, you know you're her favorite."

Vicki sighed. "Gimme a few minutes. I feel sick from eating so many pancakes."

Her cousin's stomach chose that moment to rumble.

"You need to meet Rule. He doesn't talk much, but he sure can cook."

They sat without speaking, feeling each other's exhaustion.

"The silence here is nice, you know?"

Sean nodded. "Just going to close my eyes a sec."

Vicki did too, after convincing herself she'd find a way to make Sean deal with her great-grandmother while she rescued them from the ravenous Ravagers. Smiling at her play on words, she closed her eyes for just a minute.

Or two.

Chapter Six

Dom grinned at the sour look on Eric's face. Priceless. The prime finally had a worthy female, and he didn't know how to handle her. Sure, they could keep Vicki here indefinitely. But they didn't want her unhappy. Unlike the Lawless clan, the Savages prided themselves on pleasing their females. And there was no doubt in his mind that Vicki belonged.

"Well, Prime? What do you want to do about our new guest?"

"Not a damn thing. That woman is going to accept her place. One way or the other."

The gathering menace on Eric's face should have worried him, but Dom had a feeling Vicki would hold her own. In the short time she'd been with them, she'd nearly overpowered them twice and had taken on Tommy Chen, a man known throughout the city as the leader of the Underground.

"Yeah, well, something we need to consider. Chen's after her. He won't stop because this isn't his territory. We need to find out exactly what business our female had with him."

Eric raised a brow. "Our female?"

Dom flushed and as quickly went on the offensive. "Say what you want, but you know that as your guard I'm the closest thing you have to a shadow. She's yours, yes, but that very fact makes her mine as well."

"I know. I just wanted to see if you knew it." Eric paused. "What do you really think, Dom? You told me to mark her, and I did. The sex was indescribable. But she's human. I'm not so sure I did the right thing."

"We're not talking about you claiming her, Eric." *Not yet.* "No one's going to protest you taking her as consort. The woman's a walking wet dream."

"It's bad enough we have two females in the pack who won't conform. And now Diana's marked a non-Ravager as well?" Eric swore. "She and Kate are a huge pain in my ass. They never do anything the way they're supposed to. I should have given them to another pack when they tumbled into this stale world. But no, *my guard* told me to take them in. Give them a home, a family." Eric snorted. "You're fired."

Dom ignored him. He'd been fired so many times he'd lost count. "Speaking of Kate. There's something not right about her."

"What's wrong?" Eric frowned. Though he constantly bitched about the females in their pack, he worried over them like a proverbial mother hen. "Is she sick?"

"No, not sick." Dom wasn't sure if what he thought was true. Their packmate had been putting out some strange vibes lately, and her displeasure with Jesse and Logan felt more like jealousy than real anger. An interesting dynamic that would drive Eric crazy. Best to let it lie until he knew something more concrete. "It might be nothing. Don't worry. I'll keep an eye on her. You, however, need to start paying better attention to Nev. I still think it was a mistake to let any of that clan live. Fucking integrate them already and be done with it."

Eric scratched at the table with nails that suddenly elongated, displaying his frustration. "That would make me no better than Nev. Isn't the matter of choice why we decided to break away from them in the first place?" he growled, his tone clearly unhappy. "What's with him, anyway? Talking to Chen, isn't that what the Valk said? Since when has a Lawless bastard ever reached out to a non-Ravager for help?"

Dom sighed. The boy he'd once befriended no longer existed in the crazed Nev Lawless. "He killed another human last week. I can't be certain, but I think he's attracted a few Watchers. Maybe that's why he's looking to Chen. Rumor has it Chen has his fingers in everything in Cross Step. Nev no doubt hates the bastard, but he's not stupid. He senses power and knows how to use it. Like his old man." He frowned, recalling too clearly what a hell it had been to serve in the old days.

"Shit." Eric exhaled a deep breath. "We don't need Watcher attention. Fucking human scum. You remember what they did to the Gryphs. Now there's less than a handful of them in this world. Once the Watchers latch on to Nev's shitheads, it's only a matter of time before they target us. Have Malcolm dig deeper. I want to know everything Nev's been doing for the past few weeks, why his appetite is raging out of control and what the hell Will is up to. That asshole's still keeping Kate in his sights, and I don't like it."

Dom scowled. "Neither do I. Hell, Eric. Maybe *we* should talk to Tommy Chen before Nev sinks his claws into him. If we do run into Watcher problems, Chen could be a help."

"Or turn into a bigger problem than the Watchers bent on Voider annihilation and a rabid Ravager combined. Let's keep this in-house for now, but I'll keep an ear out on Chen. Walker, our new Valk contact, is going to earn his keep." Eric paused to look at the clock above the mantle behind Dom. "I need to clean up and take care of business for the next few hours. Keep our consort occupied and out of trouble while I'm busy."

"No problem."

Eric raised a brow. "Care to wager on that?"

Dom glanced at the large crack in the table and sighed. "No, I really don't."

Eric rose from the table. "Oh and, Dom?"

"Yeah?"

"Feel free to play with our newest houseguest. But you steer clear of that pussy. You got me?"

Dom grinned at Eric's irritability. The prime wanted to bathe his consort's womb with his own seed. Sounded a lot like claiming a mate to Dom. But he liked his head attached to his body, so he choked his laughter back and nodded. "Sure thing, Prime."

"Now get out of here before I remember I fired you."

* * * * *

It took Dom longer than he'd thought to find her. She lay on her cousin's chest in the library, sound asleep. The pair of them looked enough alike to be brother and sister—the only thing saving Sean from having his throat torn out. Dom didn't like Vicki touching another male not pack, and despite Diana's obvious obsession for the male, Dom hadn't made up his mind about Sean Morely.

Footsteps fell behind him and he glanced over his shoulder to see Diana.

She sniffed and sighed. "I figured he needed a little space. Didn't think he'd actually hide from me."

"He didn't." Dom shifted so she could see into the room. "Your new toy fell asleep."

Diana shoved him with her elbow. "He's not a toy." The harsh whisper surprised him. "Sean's mine. Marked and soon claimed."

He raised a brow. "Something you need to clear with Eric first."

"He didn't clear *her* with me or Kate," she muttered. Then, as if realizing her disrespect, she flushed and glanced away.

"Good thing Prime didn't hear that, little sister." Dom bared his teeth and entered the room. He took Vicki in his arms and walked out with her as Diana took care of Sean.

Anticipating a fight, he didn't know what to do with her when Vicki's breath brushed his throat and she snuggled closer in his arms. Giving in to temptation, he took her to the room he shared with Eric and laid her down on the bed.

Asleep, she looked both innocent and seductive. The flush of her lashes against her cheeks made crescent shadows and showed her exhaustion. Yet each rise and fall of her chest reminded Dom of the bounty beneath, full breasts with dusky red nipples even now peaking in response to his arousal.

He swore beneath his breath. Now that Vicki was marked, she'd feed off her pack's desire whenever in close proximity. As she was doing now. Fuck him if the scent of her rising need didn't push his through the roof.

He took off his clothing in a rush, releasing the pressure over his aching cock. He slid his thumb over his slit, amused to find himself wet. Vicki would suit Eric perfectly; He knew because she suited *him* perfectly. Few females had ever kept his interest for longer than a few days. He instinctively sensed Vicki was different.

With slow, deliberate patience, he unbuttoned her shirt and slid it off her body. By the Void, the sight of such soft skin covering strong, lean muscle aroused his need to possess. The pull of her unique energy gave him a hard-on, and he thanked clan interference for giving him this alone time with Vicki. Though he wanted to experience the bliss of coming inside her warm pussy, they needed to come to an understanding so she would better know how to deal with Eric. Dom was just the Ravager to teach her.

Grinning with anticipation, he continued to remove every stitch of her clothing until she lay naked on his bed. She stretched like a cat and sighed. Before she could curl away from him, he leaned close and closed his mouth around her tight nipple.

She froze and as quickly relaxed, melting under him. He sucked on the ripe bud in his mouth, teasing and nipping. Vicki rewarded him by shifting restlessly under his touch. Almost awake but not quite.

He toyed with her other breast, alternating his tongue and fingers until she moaned in pleasure.

"Oh God. Not a dream," she said thickly as she blinked at him. "What are you doing to me?"

"What do you think?" Dom trailed kisses down her abdomen and continued to her sweet, moist sex. "So damn wet for me. I like that." He licked her with a firm tongue, gratified by her muffled shout.

"Dammit, Dom. Let me go," she breathed. But the firm grip she had on his hair told him otherwise.

He sucked on her clit, hungry for more. He throbbed, aching to release. Dom knew if he bathed Vicki's womb with seed, Eric would tear him a new one. But there were other ways to play.

She eased up on his hair and ran her fingers through it in a caress that made him shiver. Ravagers loved physical contact, and they especially loved being petted.

He groaned and sucked harder, thrusting a finger inside her tight sheath.

She cried out his name, so he added another finger, widening her. She'd need to adapt quickly to sate Prime, which made him wonder…

He withdrew his fingers, now slick with her cream, and rimmed her asshole with it.

She didn't protest but he felt her tense all the same.

"Never been taken here, eh?" he asked as he kissed the slick folds of her sex.

He didn't push. There would be time enough for that later. Now he needed to come.

Dom kissed her once more then lay next to her. "Get up on your hands and knees and turn around."

"I think—"

"Don't think. Just do," he growled and yanked her over him. "I'm gonna come inside you one way or the other. That hot mouth or that tight, virgin ass? Your choice."

Her eyes brightened with anger and more than a hint of lust. She wanted him, as badly as he wanted her. To punish him, she sealed their mouths together, aggressive as she dominated the kiss. The challenge wasn't lost on Dom, and it only increased his need to handle her.

"You can't do this to Prime," he managed when she ran her mouth over his neck. She bit him hard and rubbed against his cock with a snaking insistence. He groaned and concentrated on not coming. "You little witch, turn around."

He thrust his tongue in her mouth and delved between her legs with a seeking finger that found her clit and stayed there. She writhed against him, seeking ease from the same buildup growing inside him. The passion flared hot between them, a prelude to what she'd be like between him and his prime, finally filling that restlessness that had come to plague Eric for too long.

Dom tore his mouth free. "Turn the fuck around."

She didn't argue, and in seconds he stared up at a wet, hot pussy. He drew her hips down and latched on to her clit at the same time she engulfed his cock.

Intense didn't describe the feelings coursing through him. Excitement, a rising need and an unfathomable tie to this human woman confounded his *guer*, even as it dared his warrior's spirit to tangle with her.

Dom was aware of his growling, of her moans and gasps of pleasure. Only Vicki mattered now.

He thrust a finger inside her as he licked and sucked with desperation. Needing to consume her, he increased the pressure over her clit as the fire burning him from the inside out spiraled through his balls and upward.

She fondled his sac and stroked the base of his shaft as she devoured him. The heat was indescribable as he tensed and finally poured himself into her. With his teeth now fully lengthened, he scraped one across her clit and shot her into an orgasm as well.

How the vixen had outlasted him, he didn't know, but he continued to come as she gulped him down in greedy swallows, stirred by her own powerful release.

When their shudders stopped, they let go of one another. Vicki turned around and straddled his waist. Her breasts heaved and her tight nipples stood at attention, so flushed and pretty under his regard.

There's no question. She's the one. His *guer* settled as Vicki stroked him first with her gaze and then her hands. The need to protect, to cherish, settled over him. Like most Ravager females needing to claim their males, Vicki's *guer* had begun to attract the beginning of a pack—*him*. Oh hell, Eric was going to just *love* this. But right now, Dom couldn't dwell on his prime's reactions. His female was stroking him, showing her pleasure. He basked in it.

She ran her fingers over his sculpted chest, his shoulders and his upper arms. "You're so strong. All of you are big, but you and Eric, you're so…"

"He's Prime. I'm his guard. The strongest lead," he explained in a husky voice.

"Jesse and Logan? Kate and Diana? What about them?"

Dom closed his eyes in sheer bliss. She'd begun petting his hair again, sliding strands of it through her fingers.

"Dom?"

He blinked. "Our *guer*, the fierce spirit inside us, can sense compatibility. Jesse and Logan fit Prime, for now." *But not for much longer.*

"And the females?"

Was it his imagination, or did she seem a bit jealous? He made a note to mention it to Eric. "Kate and Diana are with us because we can keep them safe. Eric knows this, but he needed a reason to take them on. The females haven't claimed mates yet, and they've never had sex within their pack."

She nodded, seeming completely at ease while having a conversation with him naked. Most humans, in his experience, had a sense of overrated modesty, a self-consciousness about the human form. But not his Vicki.

He grinned.

"What are you smiling at?" she asked and smiled back.

"Those pretty tits," he grumbled. "Lean closer so I can taste."

She lowered herself and sighed with pleasure when Dom sucked both peaks. "I'm only letting you get what you want because you gave me one hell of an orgasm. And they're breasts, not tits."

"Hmm." He didn't care. He'd grown hard again. He wanted more.

"Oh no," she said and scrambled off him. "You took advantage once. Not again."

She delighted him. He could smell her need, could feel it in the trembling bonds slowly forming between them. And still, she fought. A fitting mate.

"You know, you need to get used to fucking whenever you want it. There's no shame in expressing a connection physically."

She blushed. "Yeah, well. I have male friends, but I don't screw any of them as a way of saying hello."

"Good. Because any male other than Prime or me is now off-limits."

Vicki glared. "Hold that thought. I'm going to shower, dress—in my own clothes you're going to get for me from Logan—then explain to you how incredibly wrong you really are. And it's been an hour," she said with a sniff. "I'm still waiting for my apology."

Dom watched her flounce into the adjoining bathroom and slam the door. She'd dismissed him. Dominic Savage, guard to the Ravager Prime, ignored by a human female. He laughed at the absurdness of it and was still chuckling when he tossed her a set of clothing, deliberately holding off on a bra, through the door. Logan had put her things in Eric's armoire, where they belonged.

Vicki left the bathroom fully dressed in a pair of jeans and a soft blue t-shirt. "Well?"

"Well, what?" he asked.

"Aren't you going to clean up?"

He stood, pleased when her gaze immediately sought his thick erection. "I'd rather you licked me clean."

An answering heat darkened her eyes. "I'll...I'll wait for you." She moved to the other side of the bed and sat in a stuffed leather chair. "Now hurry up."

Stubborn to the last. He shook his head. "That's right. Wait for me right here." His order, not her decision. "There are some things we need to discuss. And Vicki? If I come out and you're not here..."

She raised a brow.

"We'll make your ass reaming happen sooner rather than later. Wherever I find you, you'll drop and give it to me. Hear me?"

Her jaw dropped and her eyes widened, first with incredulity, then fury. "You son of a bitch."

"See you soon." He shut the bathroom door on her fuming face then looked sorrowfully at his cock, which only grew harder when Vicki turned on the rage. *Sorry, beast, more sex will have to wait. Knowing our Conduit, she can hold on to a mad for an entire day. Damn. I think Eric might be right about me turning human. I think I'm falling in love.*

Chapter Seven
ಸಾ

Vicki stared at the closed door in horror. Being taken in the ass wasn't something she looked forward to, but if he caught her here on the property... Taken in front of a group of sexually starved Voiders wasn't her idea of a good time. If only she could put a lid on her horny libido, because a part of her *wanted* everyone to know Eric and Dom desired her.

How sick am I? And how the hell is Ravager nookie going to bring me the husband and kids I want? This is so not the path to happily ever after.

She shrugged off her weird sex cravings and wondered what the hell to make of this morning—from her threat in the conference room, where she felt she'd actually gained some ground, to becoming a Ravager sex toy in a hot sixty-nine she wanted to do all over again.

How the hell would she be able to go back to normal sex with normal men after this?

Just thinking about deep throating Dom again, or heaven help her, Eric, made her wet. And when the hell had she become so gifted at sucking cock? Yet she'd taken Dom like a pro. Vicki's face felt on fire. Had to be Ravager pheromones.

She'd been dreaming about Eric and Dom when Dom had intruded on her innocent enough fantasy. From walking in the woods with two handsome men to having her nipples sucked. Not a bad way to wake up, she thought with a grin. But her smile faded as she recalled how hungry Dom had made her, how easily he'd breached her control and *owned* her emotions.

Bad enough the sex kept getting better. But she'd swear she felt an alien resonance deep within her. A wildness she'd sensed in Ravagers before but that she could now feel purring within herself.

Crazy talk. Or was it?

Dom stepped out of the bathroom naked, his slick blond hair darker when wet. In no hurry, he donned a pair of boxers, jeans and a shirt. To distract herself from jumping him again, she blurted, "Why are you blond?"

He ran a comb through his hair. "Genetics."

"Duh. I meant, why are you fair when most of the clan is dark? You're the only blond I've seen, and Eric is the only one who doesn't have brown eyes."

Dom nodded and stood. "Yes. That blue is distinctive, isn't it? He's from a very strong line of Ravagers back home. My family has always been a bit different. We're all light, all a little weird too."

He smiled but he *felt* odd, almost sad, and she didn't like it. She changed the subject. "How come you guys don't go around all day in Ravager form like those outside town? The Lawless clan, right?"

His gaze narrowed and he dug his toes into thick carpeting.

Come to think of it, none of the Ravagers she'd seen yesterday had worn shoes. How bizarre.

Dom nodded to the door and they left.

Outside his room, he answered her. "Nev Lawless is a bastard who should never have been allowed off the homeworld. His family killed and oppressed more Ravagers than any humans or Watcher groups ever have."

She frowned. "I thought the Watchers were just urban myth."

"I wish."

She followed him downstairs and sat with him in the kitchen, where Rule once again toiled behind the stove, this time in a rumpled Grateful Dead t-shirt.

Dom didn't have to ask. Rule slid a plate of steak in front of him.

"Steak for him, pancakes for the rest of us?"

Rule rubbed his hands together. "For the prime's consort, steak's the least of what I can do. How about a filet rolled in bacon and peppercorns? A nice cornbread dressing on the side?"

For lunch? I'm lucky to get that at dinner. "Forget I said anything." She turned back to Dom. She didn't question her need to avoid discussing her place in the Ravager "homestead". Resolving to keep to this tentative peace until she had her questions answered, she'd learn as much about these Voiders as she could. "So, Dom, what do you do around here?"

Rule snorted. "Do? He eats. That's what he does."

Dom chuckled and continued to do just that. "Rule's just jealous because I'm prettier than he is."

"Dick."

"Ass." Dom smiled at Vicki. "My job is a simple one. I take care of the prime."

"Your king. Eric."

"That's him."

"He needs constant care? What, like a two-year old?" she asked waspishly.

"Eric can protect himself. I just help take care of his needs now and then, since he's so busy caring for everyone else." Dom frowned but she saw Rule try to hide a grin as he turned back to his stove.

"He's going to need to beat that stubborn out of you."

"Him and what army?" she dared. Beat her? Not if they wanted to live to see tomorrow. Her energy seethed, wanting an outlet.

"Prickly little thing, aren't you?" Dom teased. Instead of insulting, his tone sounded admiring. Then she recalled how he and the others had encouraged her to fight. Maybe if she played meek and submissive, they'd lose interest.

"If you say so." She had to grit her teeth to sound meek. No way she could pretend, not for a minute. "Jackass."

Dom snickered. "Can't do it, can you? Nice isn't in your vocabulary."

"Oh, I don't know. I was pretty nice to you earlier," she said in a throaty voice, one that had Dom's brown eyes darkening to black. She noticed Rule's sudden attention as well. The shift in power pleased her, and she grinned. "Now what were you saying about having to bottle feed and burp your prime?"

Dom scowled. "That's not funny, dammit. Rule, you laugh, so help me, I'm shoving your head through that vent." He turned to Vicki. "And you, I think it's time you realized just where you are and who you're with."

"I know who I'm with. I'm with a bunch of Ravagers on a Monday afternoon, when I'm supposed to be home with Gran for dinner tonight. I need a phone. *Right now*," she added when Dom just stared at her as if she'd grown another head.

"Look, my great-grandmother is ninety-six years old, and a bigger pain in the ass you've never met in your life. I love her to pieces, but if I don't show up for dinner, she'll skin me alive. The woman is scary, trust me." *A monstrous mind is a terrible thing to waste*, Gran liked to say, just before dangling her naughty great-grandchildren in the air with *a thought*. Prognostication, telepathy, telekinesis, Gran could do all manner of things with her mind, and she had no problem demonstrating her displeasure with any of her family when the notion hit. It was lucky the old woman loved them all too much to ever cause harm.

"I'll talk to her for you," Dom said smoothly. "No need for her to worry when she doesn't see you for a while."

Vicki snorted. "Good luck with that. The woman is like a dog with a bone. Something else you have in common."

Insulting her kidnapper by referring to him as a dog wasn't smart, but she wasn't pleased with the reminder she couldn't leave the compound. She just had to figure out why her energy wasn't working the way it should. She'd put the pack on their asses at that bar. So how the hell had they used it against her here?

Dom reached into his pocket and pulled out a cell phone, which irritated her anew. "Dial her number."

She did. He yanked the phone back out of her hand the minute she pushed send. Glaring daggers at him, Vicki listened to the conversation he set on speaker.

"Hello?" Gran said in a clear, strong voice. "Vicki, is that you?"

Dom's eyes widened. His phone, yet her gran knew it was her. "Is this Vicki's Gran?"

"Who the hell is this?"

"Oh yeah, that's Vicki's grandmother," Rule muttered.

"My name is Dominic. I was calling to let you know Vicki won't be home for dinner."

"Why can't she tell me instead?" Gran wanted to know.

"Because she's afraid of you," Dom said bluntly.

"I am not." Vicki huffed. "I'm right here, Gran. This idiot won't let me—"

"A friend of yours, eh?" Gran asked.

The woman sounded pleasant, and the hair on the back of Vicki's neck stood on end.

Gran continued. "Sounds like a fellow who might growl a lot. You growl a lot, Dom?"

"When the moon's full, sure," he answered with a grin, apparently amused at the human myth linked to his kind. "Or when I'm talking to your great-granddaughter. She's a stubborn woman."

"Just like me. She's named for me, you know."

Gran chuckled, and Vicki frowned. Gran didn't like anyone. Why the hell was the stubborn old woman warming to *Dom*?

"He's holding me here hostage. Him and his *prime*," Vicki emphasized. *Voiders, Gran. Help me out here*, she thought as hard as she could, hoping her great-grandmother would hear her.

"You're not the prime?" Disappointment speared Gran's voice.

"I'm his guard."

"So you're pack. Savage or Lawless?"

"Savage, of course."

"Good, good," Gran said. "Enjoy yourself, Vicki. And have Sean call me. He owes that poor girl an explanation for disappearing the way he did. No wonder she bit him. Idiot," she muttered and disconnected.

Vicki stared at the phone in shock.

"What's wrong? She seemed nice." Dom finished up his steak and swallowed it down with a glass of milk Rule handed him.

"That wasn't my Gran. I don't know who that was, but it wasn't Victoria Morely."

"Hey, you dialed the number."

"I know, but..." How to explain that Gran didn't think anyone was good enough for Vicki.

The stubborn woman had taken a determined interest in her daughter and each subsequent female relative with her name. Gran insisted on choosing husbands for each of her female relatives, and with her instinctive ability to read people, no one argued with the family matriarch. But in Vicki's case, Gran grew more and more intolerant. Hell, Vicki couldn't even date without an interrogation anymore, and Sean wondered why she didn't go out. Gran simply didn't think any man Vicki brought home measured up.

But she'd been pleased when talking with Dom. What the hell was the old girl up to now?

Sean chose that moment to enter the kitchen. He glared at everyone, including the women with him.

Dom said in a quiet voice, "Diana, Kate, this is Vicki, Eric's consort."

Supposedly, Eric had informed everyone in the clan about her yesterday morning. She wondered why Dom felt the need to do so again with Diana and Kate.

The women nodded at her. Diana seemed a bit more friendly, though she focused the majority of her attention on Sean. Kate, however, glared at her when Dom wasn't looking. Her venom spoke volumes. *Definitely not a fan of mine. Good. Maybe I can use that.*

Vicki nodded back. "Sean, that's Rule." She pointed at Rule hovering by the counter. "The cook."

"The only one who *can* cook," Rule said with an arrogant sniff that made Diana and Kate smile.

To Sean, Diana said in a loving voice, "Sit down, honey, I'll get you something to eat."

Rule and Dom stared at her in shock, and even Kate blinked in surprise.

"No thanks," Sean said with icy politeness. "I want to see the prime. *Now.*"

Vicki knew better to argue with Sean in this mood. It seemed even Diana sensed there'd be no reasoning with him. Using her inner sight to look at his aura, Vicki was dismayed to see it clouded with fatigue, uncertainty and that same undeniable hunger that still raced inside her.

"Cut it out," he growled at her, which had Dom and Rule, oddly enough, coming to her defense.

"Watch how you talk to Vicki," Rule rumbled.

"Unless you want to lose your tongue and the head that goes with it," Dom added. To her unease, he seemed to grow larger and hairier as he stared down at her cousin.

Sean stared into Dom's eyes a minute too long, because Dom's nails and teeth grew razor sharp. Diana took a step forward, seething with worry.

As if he realized he'd pushed as hard as he dared, Sean glanced away. "Sorry."

He didn't sound sorry, but he'd said it. Diana's sigh of relief mirrored her own.

Vicki socked him hard on the arm.

"Ow."

"Moron. Tone it down, would you? We're not exactly at home," she cautioned with a nod at Dom, who slowly resumed his more human form.

"It's been a long weekend." Sean glared at the women behind him but said nothing more.

Dom took charge. "You want to see the prime? Follow me. Come on, Kate, you too. Diana, stay here."

Diana sat without protest and stared after Sean with longing. Clearly the female cared for him.

Escaping Diana's lovesick expression, Vicki hurriedly followed the others out of the kitchen down a familiar path. Two Ravagers stood outside the conference room. She recognized one of them as Malcolm, the Ravager she'd knocked unconscious. The guards nodded to Dom in respect, and to her surprise, nodded to her as well. Malcolm, of course, added a wicked grin and a thorough appraisal as she passed by. She ignored a surprising flare of heat and glared.

Sean stood protectively at her back as they followed Dom into the conference room where the cracked table still sat.

She flushed at the result of her temper.

Reading her, Sean grinned, though the expression didn't reach his eyes. "Nice."

"You two wait here. Kate, come with me." Dom dragged her with him out through another door and handed her off to someone else. After a few words, he shut the door behind him and gestured at the table. "Please, sit."

"Sure, let's be civilized about this," Sean said, sarcasm evident in his tone. "Look, Savage. Vicki and I have a business to run. We aren't marked, no matter what the fuck Diana and you think." Sean looked at Vicki, his expression darkening when he saw the bruise on her throat, one that appeared a mirror image of the one he'd had yesterday on his own neck.

"It's not a matter of thinking it, Sean. It's done. Our chemical stimulant has already entered your bloodstreams. You feel the psychic press upon your senses, the roar of *guer* that boils beneath your skin unless you satisfy the cravings." Much of what Dom said didn't make sense, but the intensity of his words intrigued her. "That wildness needs to feed. You're both Conduits, gifted with power many of your kind will never understand. If you don't feed it, if you don't exercise your gift, it consumes you, am I right?"

"Your point?" Sean asked through gritted teeth.

"His point," Eric said as he entered the room, "is that you now belong to us. You're pack for as long as we own you. Salinas will look the other way. They don't want trouble. Your government in the States won't interfere either. They haven't acknowledged your existence in over fifty years," he said with disgust. "No loyalty there. But here you'll be treated as family. Here you'll be able to quench the fire burning in your belly. No reprisal, no judgment or scorn for being the animal you truly are. Why would you possibly fight this?"

"Because it wasn't my choice to be here." Sean's voice rose with each word.

"You don't like Diana?"

"I like Diana just fine, but I never asked to be marked. Or claimed," he muttered.

"Claimed?" Eric sought Dom for confirmation.

Dom nodded.

"I'll talk to her." He didn't look happy about the pronouncement, and Sean seized on his discontent.

"Don't bother. Look, you're prime. I get it. I'm not trying to screw with your authority. Just let me and Vicki out of here and—"

"*No*. Vicki's mine."

"The hell she is." Sean's eyes glowed, a sure sign of trouble brewing. Energy flared around him, licking at Vicki to join in.

She did, but only to calm him. Placing a hand on his shoulder, she tried to pull away the violent energy of anger. "Sean, easy. Not like this. Gran wouldn't like it. She wants you to call her, by the way."

Mention of their great-grandmother did the trick. "What?" His anger fizzled, but before he could ask more, Dom had him by the throat.

"You do not threaten the prime and live."

She stared agog at the lethal predator holding her two-hundred-plus-pound cousin off the floor. Not an hour ago Dom had been giving her pleasure beyond belief. Right now, Sean dangled like a rag doll from his clawed hand as Dom closed off his airway.

"Dom, stop!"

Eric watched dispassionately, but when he turned to regard Vicki, his eyes burned with anger. "Well, Vicki? Are you mine or aren't you? Make it easy for your cousin to understand."

The prick. "Another choice, hmm? First the Salinas, now my cousin. Fine, I'm all yours," she snarled and stepped right up into his face. "But be careful what you wish for. You harm one more hair on my cousin's head, I'll carve your balls from your body, *Prime*."

For some ungodly reason, the scent of him turned her on despite her anger.

Eric confounded her by smiling. "Perfect. Dom, easy. Don't hurt our new packmate. Diana wouldn't be pleased." He whistled.

Jesse and Logan opened the door and stepped inside the room.

"Hey, Vicki," Jesse said with a smile. He caught Sean when Dom tossed him. "We missed you."

"We did," Logan agreed and grabbed Sean's other arm, holding her sagging cousin between them. "What say we meet up in my bedroom in a few hours? You can show me that thing you do with your tongue again." He wiggled his eyebrows and smiled, so charming she smiled back as she flipped him off.

"In your dreams, furball."

"A pet name. I told you she likes me better," he said to Jesse.

Something growled outside and everyone turned to the door.

Jesse blinked in bewilderment at the doorway through which he'd come. "What the hell is her problem?" he asked no one in particular.

"Oh hell. How long does the stubborn woman think this can go on?" Dom excused himself.

Eric gestured to Jesse and Logan. "Before you two go on break, take Sean back to Diana's room. *Gently*," he added when Vicki continued to frown at him. "Vicki and I have a few more things to discuss. She's got a long day ahead of her."

The naughty expressions that lit their faces warned her to be wary, but to her bemusement, they glanced out the door, away from her.

"Yes, Prime," Logan said with sigh and left with Jesse and Sean.

Great. What can I expect today? Another orgy? Or maybe they'll throw me to whatever — whoever — growled and watch the bloodfest.

"I'd love to know what you're thinking," Eric murmured as he approached. He stood close and sniffed. "I take it Dom gave you the tour this morning?" To her astonishment, he dropped to his knees and stuck his face in her crotch. "Good man." He stood and kissed the breath out of her, licking her lips and stroking her tongue with a promise of more to come.

"What the hell was that about?" she asked when she could catch her breath.

"Just checking on something. Now let's clear up a few things before we get to the good stuff." He seated her at the cracked table and sat uncomfortably close.

The direction of his perusal, which lingered on her breasts, told her what to expect, but she couldn't stop herself from asking. "Get to the good stuff?"

"Before I fuck you until you can't walk. And then we'll all do it again. And again."

"We all?" she said weakly.

"My marker is there, but it's new. It needs to be stronger. Another few rounds with the four of us should do the trick. Then it's just you, me and Dom." He grinned, showing her sharp white teeth. "There's a hierarchy. You're mine, and as such, you belong to my guard too. He's mine."

Don't ask. "Jesse and Logan?"

He shrugged. "Part of my pack, but they're healthy, unclaimed males. They don't belong to me or a female."

"What?"

"My *guer* isn't tied to them, not the way it is to Dom." He frowned. "Look, if you'd prefer we mark you again in private, rather than publicly as most Ravagers do, you need to talk now. I'm through waiting."

"We are talking."

"I suggest you tell me about Chen and what you—"

"I'll tell you what you can do with your suggestions—"

"Malcolm?" Eric called.

"Prime?" Malcolm entered from the front doorway he'd been guarding.

"I'm sure Malcolm would be more than happy to watch while I prepare your sweet little ass for penetration."

She could feel herself blushing. "*Talk*, you bastard," she grumbled half under her breath.

"Never mind, Malcolm."

"Damn." Malcolm left, but not after asking Eric, "Maybe later?"

Eric chuckled. He sobered after meeting Vicki's furious stare. "Tell me what the hell you took from Tommy Chen that has his men scouring the city for you. And make it fast. I'm hungry, and I need to be fed."

"You can take your appetite and go to hell." She itched to toss his ass back against the wall, her power greedily absorbing the sexual energy he exuded all the time, even without touching him.

Eric leaned closer over the table, until they touched nose to nose. "You use that sexy energy against me and I'll make you *beg* for a taste of me. You know I can."

Begging any man wasn't something she looked forward to, but begging this man—this Ravager—who'd kidnapped her rubbed her the wrong way. Especially because some stupid part of her wanted a man strong enough to reduce her to whimpers. No, not just any man. Eric. *God, I need my head examined.*

"Vicki?" He put his hand around her throat and gently squeezed.

To her horror, her panties grew damp. Her clit pulsed and her breasts ached. She cursed him in her mind while answering in a rush. "It all started a few months ago, when a client came to us wanting to recover a family heirloom. There's this ring..."

Chapter Eight

೧೦

Kate glared through tears as she stormed from the house. That bitch. Who the hell did she think she was flirting with Savage men? Jesse and Logan were *hers*, dammit. For years she'd stood by, playing the little sister to Diana. Not tied by birth but by love, she and Diana had deeper bonds than blood. But with Diana enthralled with Sean, things had changed.

Kate didn't feel a part of their magic. Pack was pack, but Diana would be breaking off, starting her own family. Problem was her human didn't seem to want to be a part of it. Poor Diana. Kate knew how it hurt to be denied. For years she'd loved Jesse and Logan, but they saw nothing but Eric and what Eric wanted.

Granted, she loved Eric. Like a big brother or benevolent uncle, but never as a lover. He felt the same way. He'd prodded her and Diana for years to take mates and start their own packs, not out of a desire to be rid of them, but so that they might experience true happiness. She hadn't the heart to tell him who she really wanted. She thought Diana might suspect, but she'd never said anything.

Kate didn't know what to do. She didn't want Vicki around at all. It was hard enough sharing her men with Dom and Eric. Ravagers didn't care about gender when it came to sex, but she hated being near and unable to satisfy the Ravagers she knew would make perfect mates. Her *guer* warned her that Vicki would make a formidable adversary. Human she might be, but Conduits had their own power. Kate had seen Sean in action. Was his cousin as strong?

She hoped so. Kate wanted to beat her fairly. If she couldn't, though, so be it.

She sensed Dom closing on her. Best to let him catch up and say what he needed to say.

"Kate, stop," Dom growled at her. Instead of berating her for daring to warn off the prime's consort, he opened his arms and hugged her. "You're old enough now to do something about it, you know." He kissed the top of her head, and fresh tears started anew.

"I don't know what you mean."

"Honey, I see everything around here. That's my job. Now tell me why you won't declare yourself to your packmates who would rather die than hurt you?"

She sniffed. "But that's just it. I shouldn't have to declare myself. They don't notice anything but Eric and you and now *that woman*."

She felt his smile against her hair and struggled in his arms. "It's not funny!"

"No, it's not. But if it's any consolation, Vicki didn't ask to be here, Kate. She's trying to fit in as best she can. It would be nice if she had someone to help her."

Someone to help her leave, maybe. That way Kate wouldn't have to deal with the obnoxious human. The way she flaunted herself, challenging the males clearly to entice them. It made Kate sick.

"You're right. I'm sorry." Kate gave Dom her best smile, the one that showed off her dimple.

He bought it, probably relieved not to have to deal with female issues any more. She'd overheard him and Eric complaining about her and Diana for years. Always with love in their voices, yet they didn't want the responsibility for two extra females in their pack. And who could blame them?

"I'm okay now. I'll apologize to Vicki later, hmm?"

"Good girl."

Woman, I'm a woman, she wanted to shout. "I'm just going for a run to clear my thoughts. I'll be back soon." She eyed her watch, needing to leave now if she wanted to see them again. She forced a smile to her face and waved at Dom.

As soon as he left, she hurried into the tree line and stripped off her clothes. Shifting into her *guer*, she raced through the woods, passed a few of her brethren and continued on. There, by the small stream of water, an empty bed of grass. She sniffed the air and used the direction of the wind to camouflage her scent. Then climbing a gnarled oak, one of her favorite hiding places, she waited.

Minutes later, she heard them.

Two Ravagers almost identical in their *guer* approached. So handsome, so strong.

So hers.

They stopped and changed back, disappointing her. She'd been hoping for some rough play this afternoon. Still, she could stare at them all day and not get tired.

Jesse stretched, and Logan watched him. The play of sunlight over his muscles mesmerized her, and it took a moment to realize they spoke in low tones.

"What do you think's wrong with her?"

"I don't know. Maybe Eric pissed her off." Logan shrugged. "He's good at that."

"Yeah, but she seemed more angry at Vicki than Eric."

Just the name made her want to growl.

"Why? You think Kate has a thing for Eric?" Logan asked, his voice stilted.

They were talking about her. Noticing her, finally!

"*Hell no.* Eric's like her second father. He found her and Diana."

"No shit, Jesse. I was there, remember?"

Jesse smiled, his grin smug. "Yeah, but you were just a pup then. So cute when you were little." He took a few steps closer and ran his fingers up and down Logan's abdomen. "But not so little now, eh?"

Logan drew in a sharp breath. "Why do you think Kate's so upset lately?"

"She always seems mad. Wish I knew," Jesse murmured before taking Logan in hand. He gripped Logan hard. "My turn today."

"Fuck." Logan moaned and spread his feet wide. "Then get me off first. You're a fucking tease."

Jesse chuckled. "You sound like you're needing it bad. Thinking about Vicki?" He jerked Logan off as he taunted him.

"No. Something…at the house. Making me hornier than usual."

"I thought it was just me feeling that way." He stepped closer and rubbed against Logan.

From her vantage, Kate couldn't see more than Jesse's firm backside as he pressed against Logan. It wasn't long before she heard Logan groan. His face contorted in pleasured agony, and she clenched inside, wishing she held him deep as he spent. Instead, Jesse stepped back from Logan and rubbed his lover's cum over his cock, making the slide of his palm so pretty.

"Down on your hands and knees for me," Jesse said thickly, stroking himself as he watched Logan get down. "How about a little suck first?"

"No way. You'll blow, you bastard."

Jesse chuckled.

"I'm not in the mood to swallow."

"Not what you were feeling yesterday when Dom ordered you to your knees."

She sensed but didn't see Logan blush. "I can't help it. He's so fuckin' hot. And don't tell me you've never taken it from him, or Eric for that matter. You might top me, but I've seen you bottom too. Hell, I've heard you scream out when Prime's reaming that fine ass."

Enthralled by their frank talk, Kate bit her lip as she imagined them both taking *her*. Logan and Jesse were so handsome, so fierce and so male. She watched as Jesse spread Logan's ass cheeks and thrust inside.

Logan groaned as he took each thick inch. She loved seeing the light play off their muscle, scenting the Ravager need in the air, strong and true. Unlike the humans who had to label every sexual act, Ravagers revered carnal joining. The communion her packmates shared brought them closer together. By accepting Dom, Eric and each other, they accepted their place in their family.

Except Kate wanted to start a new pack. As a female, she had the right to select her mates. But the thought of them actually accepting scared her. Any male would happily mate a Ravager female, due to so few of them being around. Kate wanted Jesse and Logan to desire her for herself, not out of a sense of duty to perpetuate the species. She wanted them to *love* her, a human reaction, but she couldn't help it. Love was the one thing she found respectable about the native species of this world.

Jesse swore as he neared his end, distracting her from pathetic thoughts.

"Fuck, Logan. You're so hot. I'm coming. That's it." He tensed. His fingernails turned into claws as he gripped Logan's hips and dug deep. Thin trails of blood dripped down Logan's sides, but Logan only groaned.

Probably coming again, Kate thought, not surprised to see his hand moving between his legs as he panted. Talk about insatiable. Logan and Jesse fucked every day out here on their break. Then they usually screwed at night if they hadn't already in the morning. Every now and then they chose to share a lone female, normally a human because other Voiders gave Ravagers a wide berth. So Kate shouldn't have been so threatened by Vicki.

But she was.

Logan grunted as he spilled over his hand, and Jesse withdrew, wiping his remaining seed on Logan's back.

"Lot of cum, pretty boy," Jesse rasped as he squeezed his cock and shook it. "Oh man, I needed that."

"I want to blame this on Eric, but it doesn't feel the same. My *guer* is tired, sated, and dammit all, still hungry," Logan growled.

He sniffed, and Jesse glanced around. "You think one of the females is going into heat?"

"I don't know, but it's high time we mentioned this to Eric. If it's affecting us, it might be screwing with some of the other males as well. We sure the hell don't need an in-house battle over a female."

Jesse shook his head. "Hey, if her males aren't satisfying her, it's our right as unclaimed to step in."

"Yeah, I know. But it just doesn't feel right. I want..." Logan rubbed the back of his neck. He stood, used the stream to clean himself while Jesse did the same, then whispered something in Jesse's ear.

"Sounds good. I'll meet you back at the house."

Logan nodded and watched his packmate disappear. When he moved off in the other direction, Kate quickly scrambled down the tree, wanting to head back on the off chance they turned around and found her lingering scent in the air.

She turned to run and stifled a scream. Jesse and Logan glared at her.

"Well, little sister? Want to explain this? Spying, of all things?" Logan asked.

Sexually frustrated and angry at being dismissed as of no consequence *again*, she yelled, "I'm not your *little sister*," and went for his throat.

* * * * *

Nev ripped out the throat of a dead deer and tossed it in the air. He watched several curs fight over it. "Tell me," he said to Will.

"Eric's new female — Chen wants a piece of her."

Nev blinked in surprise. "Really? That's interesting. I wonder what she's worth."

"To Chen or Eric?"

"Take your pick."

Will smiled. "Rumor has it Eric's declared her untouchable. He's marked the female."

"He's never marked one before. How nice for us. Taking a human should alienate the clan better than anything we could have done. Let the rest of the Savages see what a fuckup Eric truly is. Keep an eye on his human, but no touching. I don't want her on her hands and knees with a cock up her ass until Eric's here, under my thumb, to watch."

"You take all the fun out of everything," Will said with a sigh. "And Chen?"

"I want another meet with him. I've attracted enough Watcher attention to engage his interest. One of the females we slaughtered last week belonged to a Watcher leader. I just hope they don't blame *all* the Ravagers for my little mistake."

Will snickered. "This is why you're the rightful prime. You take what you want when you want. Leaders rule from the front, not from behind Salinas skirts."

"Exactly."

Will left to take care of business. Now Nev just had to sit back and wait.

The future of the Ravagers depended upon Lawless solidarity. He ruled his clan through fear, just as his father had so many years ago. The concept worked, so why fix what wasn't broken? He'd never understood why Eric had separated, changing what made the Ravagers such a powerhouse.

Then again, in this bland world, the harsh realities of life and death were often swept under humanity's moralistic rug. Vengeance and rules were made by a governing body of assholes "elected" to office. Elected—those who bought their way in. Humans used money the way Ravagers used their claws. Unfortunately for Nev, he didn't have the skills necessary to accumulate wealth in this place. Eric did.

When the Ravagers should have stuck together and turned the world inside out to suit them and their needs, a bunch of irreverent pricks pulled away and created their own clan. Weakening the Ravagers, Eric and the Savages had destroyed what should have been a new world order.

Now females bred fewer litters, and the power in one's *guer* meant less in social spheres than a Ravager's ability to *adapt*. Utter bullshit.

Eric's policies to accept human laws, as well as female mates of any species, made him one of *them*. A fucking pussy too afraid of humans to do what he knew was right. Respect for tradition and strength no longer existed in the Savage clan. Hell, even the females in Eric's pack had yet to declare their own mates, hurting more than helping Ravager numbers, in essence facilitating the gradual decline in Ravager strength. No wonder Nev's people were dying out. They needed him. Instead, they had Eric Savage to lead them.

Nev's anger at all he'd lost since being forced into this hellish world fired his belly. It took discipline not to rush over to the Savage clan and kill as many as he could. He would time his next attack perfectly. And maybe, just maybe, he'd find what else had been stolen from him so long ago.

"Fuck you, Eric. And fuck your little pet guard too." *Soon enough, you'll bow to me again, Dom. See if you don't.*

* * * * *

Eric didn't want to believe what he was hearing. It was sheer insanity. "You're telling me you stole Tommy Chen's trademark ring because some mystery female commissioned you to?"

"You don't have to talk down to me." The foolish woman glared at him, her eyes a bright, sunny shade of yellow. "Sean and I have to work for a living, your kingship. Neither of us likes Chen anyway. He's the reason there's so much crime in the city."

Eric didn't think it the time to argue what he knew to be the truth, so he ignored her incorrectly conceived notions of Cross Step's inner workings. "Tell me again how you planned to dodge Chen after stealing his *most prized* possession."

She squirmed in her seat and glanced away. First intelligent thing she'd done all morning — make that afternoon.

"I'm waiting."

"I was going to work him over with my ability. It would have worked if the Salinas hadn't busted into the club."

"Explain 'work him over'."

She rolled her eyes. "I distract him with a few kisses, amp up his sexual energy, then fog his mind until we leave. He's out a ring and none the wiser."

The thought of Vicki kissing anyone without Eric's permission made him see red. He *owned* her. "What happened, exactly?"

"I kissed him, took the ring, then the Salinas invaded. The spell, if you will, was broken. Chen knew exactly what I did, and a ton of people saw me take down Mei Lin too, so no hiding that." She explained how she and Sean had wormed their way into the club by appealing to Chen's intrigue with females who could brawl.

After pondering the situation, Eric came to the obvious conclusion. "Give Chen back his ring, apologize and I'll settle things between you."

"Hell, no." Vicki fumed. "I worked for that ring. Sean and I stole it fairly. Besides, it's already gone. We used a broker all but one time. I have no idea who my client actually was except that she's female. I saw the back of her head just once."

"Now I have Chen to deal with? Terrific." He put his head in his hands so he wouldn't give in to temptation and strangle Vicki. Damn woman needed a keeper. Good thing he'd found her.

Vicki glared. "No, you do *not* have Chen to deal with. Sean and I will handle him. I've put up with this marking nonsense long enough. Let me and my cousin go free and I promise not to take legal action against you."

He looked at her, incredulous. "Are you serious?"

She sighed. "No. As if anyone would tangle with Ravagers. I just want to go home, Eric. You can't keep me here forever," she said quietly.

"Not forever, just long enough..." To what? he asked himself. *To get her out of my fucking system.* He couldn't explain how, but earlier, while Dom had pleasured her, he sensed the same enjoyment from both of them, but in a muted way. He'd never before heard of Ravagers sharing feelings unless they mated. He could understand experiencing Dom's sensations, but Vicki's?

"I'm waiting." Vicki tapped the desktop with nails bitten to the quick.

He laughed at her temerity. "Wait all you want. In case it's escaped your notice, I'm the fucking prime." He flashed his fangs at her, intent on a little intimidation...when she did something to him that made him groan in pleasure.

The little witch wrapped her hand around his wrist and snaked his energy, manipulating it somehow. Though he'd realigned his *guer* to shield himself before, apparently his fighting spirit no longer considered her a threat. Hell, if she weren't human, he'd think she'd begun a female's claiming rite.

The show of power only made him that much harder. As it was, just being around her turned his dick into a steel pole.

A female who could not only defy him, but had no fear of him was a challenge he couldn't resist.

"Don't threaten me, *Prime*." She showed her own teeth—pretty, white and straight. So human. Fragile yet...not. "Let me see it," she whispered and licked her lower lip. "Show me that huge cock."

Under her control, he stood, opened his trousers and took himself out.

"You see, Prime, you're not all powerful. Just horny, like most men I know." She snorted with derision, but the hunger in her voice made him throb. "Make yourself come. Go ahead. Let me watch while you stroke it."

Though he knew she'd taken hold of his senses, Eric was powerless to refuse her. But he knew one thing she didn't—*his lust enflamed her own.* He doubted she knew what she did when she absently removed her t-shirt and ran her fingers over her nipples.

Her gaze caught by his thickening erection, she breathed faster. "Hold it out; let me see it. That's it."

Caught in her own damn trap. Perfect.

"Now what?" he murmured, holding himself for her.

She let go of his wrist to run her other hand down the front of her pants.

So fucking sexy. He asked in a thick voice, "Want to lick it and see if I'm as wet as I look?"

"Mmm." She leaned close and placed her tongue at his slit. He'd never seen anything so erotic.

"Show me those tits again and I'll show you how hot you make me. Won't take me long." And it wouldn't. Just thinking about Vicki's cleavage made him stiff. Maybe she had a point about him being perpetually horny.

"Would you like to come over me? To mark me with your cum?" she rasped and leaned back. Her pretty nipples were tight and dark.

"Yeah, all over you. Baby, lay back on the desk. You know, the one you cracked." To his delight, his Conduit seemed to have forgotten all about giving him orders. "That's it," he crooned as he crawled onto the table and positioned himself over her. "Push your tits together so I can fuck them." He slid the pre-cum from his slit over his cock, to lube himself, and thrust between her mounds, feeling every touch of her smooth flesh over him. Heaven and hell in every stroke.

Hot and hard and ready to burst, he shafted her a few more times before deliberately slowing down. "Want to taste it?"

"Yeah," she breathed.

"Open up."

She opened her mouth, and he raised himself to thrust between her lips. Fucking her mouth with shallow thrusts nearly undid him. Coated with her saliva, his dick slid effortlessly between her lips.

"I'm gonna come all over you," he growled. One more thrust and he pulled away, taking care to spend over both nipples. Shining with his seed, her breasts heaved as she fought her own desires.

"You need to come now, don't you?" he asked in a hoarse voice.

"Please." She rubbed his cum into her skin.

"That's it, baby. Wipe my scent all over you."

He helped her, pulling on her nipples as he did so. *By the Void*, her breasts were perfect. Lost in her desire, she didn't protest when he took off the rest of her clothes and spread her thighs. He held her open, wanting her scent to permeate the room.

Vicki didn't blink when Eric lowered his head and nuzzled her folds. Drugged on the passion surging between them, she waited, caught in his thrall.

"You're marked and *you're mine*, you little witch," he whispered. "I can do anything I like with you."

Her eyes sparked with rebellion, and he groaned, loving the fight she never seemed without. Even now, when a normal human would have totally succumbed to a Ravager's desire, Vicki tried to mutiny.

Ravager cum was potent. Most humans would do anything to taste it. Vicki had already been dosed with it when she'd swallowed Jesse and Logan, and again with Dom. Unloading inside her had been the ultimate in ownership. But Eric wanted more.

"I'm going to suck that cunt, Vicki. To taste what I now own."

She groaned and clenched her fingers in his hair, but she didn't protest.

Vicki responded to his mouth with undiluted desire. To his surprise, her natural sensuality ensnared him as if she were a true Ravager. He could almost imagine her *guer* pulling at his, as if trying to claim him.

He licked and sucked, even shoved a finger inside her as he gave her the ultimate in oral pleasure. Each taste bound them closer together. Their scents mingled and became one. His cum saturated her skin. Her cream lingered on his tongue, sweet and perfect, the final piece of a puzzle now complete.

Shoving his tongue inside her, he licked and retreated, wanting more. He wanted to smell his seed here, to know it entered her body and coated *his* womb. He could easily imagine her round with his babe, and the thought shocked him. The Ravager prime and a human mate to carry his child? No one would accept such a joining.

But his body's demands overcame his senses. He sucked her clit while adding another finger deep inside her. Vicki screamed as she came hard. Unable to stop himself, Eric mounted her and thrust deep.

He rocked into her with a savagery he'd never before felt, a primal urge to take possession of this treasure who belonged to him and him alone. Thoughts of pack, of the clan and his responsibilities faded as he climaxed inside his woman.

He seized in a huge nova of bliss, caught in the strength of passion magnified by his very own Conduit.

She cried his name as she rode her orgasm and his, clenching him with a tight, greedy pussy.

It took him several moments to come down from his high, and when he did, he swore. Vicki had passed out from the intensity of their joining, and if he wasn't mistaken, the damn woman wore his sigil on her left breast, where he'd first jetted his seed against her. The scent of Savage Prime was strong there. It would never fade.

I've claimed a human.

Despite his strides with the clan, there were many who itched for a reason to return to Nev and his bunch. Eric liked change, but he also respected the past, wanting his heritage to remain alive in his brethren and in their progeny. Female Ravagers claimed their males. The women held the power in their packs, and in that Eric held fast to tradition.

The only male able to claim a female was the prime, whose duty to claim a *suitable* female would lead to prosperity among the clan. Custom held that only a true Ravager queen could enhance the fertility in the females of her clan. The Ravagers hadn't had a true queen in decades, not since they'd landed in this foreign world.

Female births were almost nil. Most of their women came through the Voids, and even those were few and far between.

Claiming a human as his mate would surely be a sign he'd gone over the edge.

Another thought struck him, and he staggered with the force of the stressful blow.

Could Vicki ever bear his children? And if so, would they be Ravager or something else?

That above all needed to be addressed. *Motherfucker, I knew she was going to be trouble.*

Eric withdrew from his new mate and sat beside her on the table. He clutched his temples and groaned but couldn't resist a glance at Vicki's naked body sprawled beside him. Her breasts rose and fell with every breath. She lay open, vulnerable, fully his to do with whatever he wanted.

His cock hardened as if he hadn't just filled her with enough seed to repopulate the entire Ravager species. He wanted her again, right now. But this time he'd take her ass before Dom could get to it. Clan politics, heirs, his entire existence ceased to matter next to Vicki's arousing essence.

Lost in a fogging desire, Eric leaned over her, intent on taking her again when he caught his scent powerfully strong. *Too* strong. The difference shook his *guer* and woke him from his sexual enthrallment.

Holy shit.

He'd found what no one had in a very long time. A true queen.

Yet she was also a human, one who didn't exactly like it here among his kind, and who would most likely escape at the earliest opportunity.

Fuck.

He wished he understood how it had happened in the first place. From wanting to protect her, to screwing her, to claiming her, all in one powerful sexual union?

How the hell could he fix this? Worse, why didn't he want to?

Dominic.

Dom would know what to do about this. Then again, Dom had advised him to mark Vicki, resulting in a definite addiction growing more potent every time he touched her. *My human mate.* He really should have fired Dom ages ago. His guard gave fucked-up advice.

But a true queen... Could it be? Or was his *guer* just screwed up by Vicki's whacked-out energy?

Talk about trouble in paradise, he thought as he stroked Vicki's soft skin while she slept. Eric called for Dom via the intercom on the table and waited, trying to make sense of the chaos spreading through his pack.

Diana wanted to mate with a non-Ravager, another human.

Kate suddenly had issues that made Sean look tame.

Vicki didn't want to be owned, and now the stubborn woman owned *him*. Void love him, but if she ever found out how a real Ravager relationship worked he'd never get a moment's peace. She didn't take shit from anyone, but he liked that about her. He could only hope the rest of the clan would feel the same way. Because if they didn't, his life would be worth next to nothing when the Savages turned on him. Maybe Nev was onto something about ruling strictly through fear and intimidation. Though Eric was the strongest in the pack, he remained prime because his clan believed in what he intended for their future.

Would they feel the same about him with Vicki by his side? Because he couldn't undo what he'd done. Hell, he *wouldn't* undo it, even if he could.

Eric lowered his head, wishing again for the peace he'd found in Vicki's warm body.

"By the Voids, what else can go wrong?"

Chapter Nine

Three days later, Vicki glared at the indentation where Eric's head had lain hours ago, more than annoyed he'd closeted her inside his room with orders to stay put. She hadn't been allowed to see anyone but him since he'd taken advantage of her in that blasted conference room.

She refused to admit, even to herself, that she liked spending time with the ill-mannered werewolf.

Worse than her confinement, she'd succumbed to him two nights in a row, doing any and everything the damn Ravager demanded. For a woman reared to be independent and powerful in her own right, she was acting like nothing more than his sexual slave. Vicki wanted to blame the marking thing he'd done, but honesty compelled her to confess she'd wanted him even before he'd bitten her. The man was a walking wet dream. That *guer* he talked about made her energy sit up and take notice. Perhaps if she'd been a normal woman, she wouldn't want him so much. But Vicki was a Conduit.

Her power remained a part of her at all times, a sixth sense as important to her as seeing and hearing. Manipulating energy since she'd been old enough to walk, Vicki had grown up with an uncanny sense about people. The same reason she'd convinced Sean to take on their last client told her she'd found something special here with these Voiders, and with Eric in particular.

She rubbed the spot on her breast that burned. Her hand over it eased the sting, and the fiery hurt turned to a gentle throbbing. Nothing marred her flesh, not even a bruise, despite Eric's rough handling. But she felt a flare of alien energy all the same. *Has to be Eric's doing, the sexy, controlling bastard. I'm never going to be normal after him.*

She wanted to wail at the unfairness of it all. Despite the Morely propensity for being Conduits, her family lived happily. Every one of her relatives married for love and had the well-adjusted kids to prove it. An oddity in the human world, for sure. But that stability was something Vicki had always wanted.

Trying to date Norms hadn't worked. Her one foray into a Voider relationship had been squashed by Gran an hour into her date. The few Conduits she'd met wanted nothing to do with a woman who could control them in bed. Not one of them had been strong enough to handle her.

Not like Eric and Dom.

A part of her longed to see the aggravating Ravagers again, though she couldn't have said why. *Couldn't have said, or don't want to say?* she argued with herself. *Oh, shut up.*

She'd spent three days in this room and now knew it like the back of her hand. Eric had spent the nights with her though Dom had been absent. Apparently, Eric and Dom shared the bedroom, which led to her fantasizing about the pair having sex. Her body overheated, and she hurriedly broke *that* train of thought.

Eric had a king-plus-sized bed, a large closet, several bureaus and an armoire, which held the clothes Logan had packed for her. She wanted to cheer at the bra finally supporting her once more and turned back to her perusal of the room.

Nothing adorned the beige walls. There were no pictures, books or magazines, and if she had to watch one more episode of *Pick the Voider* on cable she thought she'd puke. Rummaging through the room, she'd hoped to find something of interest. Unfortunately, the only things she'd found made her blush. The guys had a thing for dildos.

Her heart raced, her sex quickened and her nipples rubbed said support with discomfort. *No, I am not thinking of sex and Eric, or sex and Dom, or sex with them together.*

She cleared her mind and looked in Eric's closet again. He also had a lot of clothes. Most of them casual. Apparently, the prime didn't dress like royalty. Hell, none of the Ravagers she'd seen wore anything other than jeans and t-shirts or sweatshirts. She wished she understood more about them, but without anyone to talk to, knowledge of her new "pack" remained out of reach.

As if she'd conjured him, Eric banged on the door and entered, followed by Dom.

Their familiar faces warmed her, but only because she'd been dying for company, she told herself.

Lust filled the room, and she felt as much as saw Eric's gaze travel over her body. Dom too stared at her with hunger before his nostrils flared and his eyes widened.

"Oh hell, you really did it." Dom crossed the room to stand in front of Vicki. "I smelled it as soon as I stepped into the room."

She flushed. "Hey, I took a shower."

Dom grinned. "You smell tasty, honey. Truly. But that's not what I'm talking about."

"I'm fucked." Eric groaned and shut the door behind him, then leaned back against it. He scowled at Dom. "You did this to me."

"Now, Prime. I did this *for* you. You should be thanking me, you know."

"Thanks, asshole. So tell me how I did it? How did sex turn into…this?"

"Excuse me," Vicki interrupted, at a loss. "Would someone please explain what the hell you're talking about?"

Dom answered Eric as if she hadn't spoken. "Sometimes it just happens. When a connection is as strong as the one I feel between you, between *us*, the *guer* takes what it needs."

"So you're saying my *guer* did this?" Eric frowned.

"Yes. In the same way I know things you need before you do. My *guer* responds to yours, and I think your *guer* responded to hers."

"But she's human. She doesn't have a *guer*. How can she be a true qu—consort?"

"Actually, I'm a Conduit. They're not classifying us as fully human anymore," she threw in, just to be heard.

Eric ignored her. "This is all too soon. It's only been a few days, for Christ's sake."

"Eric, you need to accept it. It's obvious to anyone with a nose. Your mark is really, really potent." Dom shifted his stance, drawing her attention to his mouthwatering erection.

Good Lord. Vicki wanted him. After three days of having marathon sex with Eric, she wanted Dom again. She'd turned into a Voider nympho. And wouldn't that make Gran so proud?

"Guys, I'm right here. I still don't get it. What's the problem? You marked me when you grabbed me Sunday. What's so different about the situation now?" *Besides the obvious, me stuck in Ravager-land without a way out, and stupid me, not really wanting one.* A thought occurred to her. "So you realize you made a mistake, is that it? No problem. Let me go and I'm outta here. No trouble at all." She smiled, ignoring the pain caused at thoughts of separating from her pack—from these Ravagers.

Dom strode to her and shocked her by ripping her shirt open.

"Hey!"

He sliced through her bra, pushed it apart, and latched on to her breast before she could move. The minute his lips closed around her nipple, she sagged in his hold as unbelievable pleasure coursed through her veins. He sucked hard, nipping her and licking the sting away. Vicki wanted to ride him, to take him deep inside her while her prime watched and hungered. God, she needed it, bad.

"Oh yeah, she even tastes like you," Dom was saying as he gently laid her down in bed.

She shivered at the feel of his large, hot hands, and then blinked up into…Eric's face? Desire burned in his gaze. He ran a finger over her nipple, stirring that blaze to life once more. Instead of joining her, he drew her shirt together and sat beside her with a sigh.

"My cock is killing me. I want her twenty-four/seven," he growled. "So what now, guard? How do I break this to the clan without them falling apart? You know as much as they hate Nev, they still cling to tradition. Hell, for that matter, so do I. She's *human*."

"Conduit," Vicki corrected him again, wishing she could think clearly beyond her glands. "Quit doing that. You touch me and I can't think. Cut it out before I zap you both," she ended on a moan, wanting Eric and Dom to touch her again. She sneaked a hand under Eric's shirt and grazed his back. With a small pull, she latched on to his energy and tugged.

Eric took a swift breath and leapt from the bed.

"Of course," Dom said with a grin, looking relieved. "Not sure why I hadn't thought of it before."

"What?" Eric sounded wary.

Vicki just wanted her head to stop spinning. She internally focused, pulling in the sexual vibes so she could untangle her needs from the powerful males surrounding her. It took some doing, and she missed most of what Eric and Dom said. Finally herself again, she rolled to her side and stood with Dom's help. "Thanks," she grumbled and pulled away.

She rooted for a new bra and shirt, not liking how vulnerable she felt at being nearly naked around the powerful Ravagers.

She took the clothing into the bathroom with her and emerged to find only Dom waiting for her.

"Where'd he go?" she asked.

"Ah, clan business. I have a few things to do as well, so I'm going to leave you with Malcolm."

"Where are Jesse and Logan? I thought they were pack, but I haven't seen them in a while." Not that she minded less attention from the Ravagers, but of the four men that supposedly "owned" her, those two were the least threatening.

"Jesse and Logan are working on a special project I assigned them." The sly grin on his face worried her. "You're going to be spending much more time with Malcolm."

"But not you or Eric?" She'd put Malcolm on his ass before. She could do it again.

"What sparked that look in your eyes, Victoria Fox?" Dom murmured. He lifted her chin and looked down, past her eyes into her soul.

Just the touch of his palm heated her sex and made her wet, hungry for *him*. Mine, she thought with an inner snarl, and blinked.

"Vicki, you're the one," he murmured, stroking her lips with his finger.

"What one?" she snapped and jerked out of his hold. *Great. Now I'm a slave to my hormones. I need therapy.*

"The one who's going to start a new way of life for us Ravagers." The evident joy on his face startled her. "Now be a good girl for Malcolm. If you're smart, you'll use him to better understand life around here, to better fit in. And I wouldn't try running. I've told Malcolm that if you try anything, he has leave to enforce discipline."

She glared. "No one lays a hand on me, Dom. I'll kill him first."

"Who said anything about a hand?" His heated perusal lingered between her legs. "If memory serves, you like a strong tongue."

She blinked, stunned and thoroughly turned-on at the suggestion Malcolm would be allowed to...to... "You can't be serious? I thought I was pack. You don't share, right?" But she'd seen instances of their orgies in the house.

"Pack, right." Dom smiled and left.

When Malcolm entered with a wide grin on his face, she cursed him and stormed out of the room. He halted her by grabbing her arm. Though he seemed a few years younger than Eric and Dom, he was just as alpha-like in his tendency to manhandle her. To her horror, her clit throbbed for attention.

"Get off."

"Easy, sweetheart. I'm not going to hurt you." The look he gave her told her what he'd rather be doing.

Do any of these wolfhounds think about anything but sex? And who the hell am I to judge, when I'm a hairsbreadth from jumping his bones?

Wincing at the feel of her wet panties, she growled at him. "You're damn right you won't hurt me. Now where's my cousin? I need to talk to Sean."

"Ah, he's unavailable right now. Diana needed some time alone with him."

"Why? What's she doing to him?" Worry gave her strength, and she subtly pulled a tendril of energy from Malcolm she hoped he wouldn't miss.

He glared and yanked her closer. "Don't." Not giving her a chance to protest, he kissed the breath out of her.

Like Dom and Eric, Malcolm tasted *right*. Raw and forceful, he ate up her resistance with little effort. When he pulled away, she wanted to cling. God knew what held her back.

"Shit." He leaned closer to smell her and nuzzled between her breasts. "If you weren't so sweet, if Dom hadn't... That scent, it's killing me." He sighed and stepped back, his erection in stark relief against his jeans, his dark brown eyes sorrowful. "It's going to be a long day."

"You said it," she agreed, trying to calm her racing heart. Dying to at least appear composed and in control of herself, she scowled. "If I can't see my cousin, I'd at least like to get out of this house for a bit. Can I do that, or do I need Prime's permission?"

Spoiling for a fight, to let go of the sexual energy buzzing through her veins, she waited.

Malcolm's pupils grew wider and darker, as if he could smell her frustration. "I—" He stopped to clear his throat and shifted on his feet. "Why don't we go outside for a walk? Far away from everyone," he added with a hoarse curse.

"Good idea."

* * * * *

"Did you see that?" Dom asked.

Eric nodded, no longer so nervous about the future thanks to Dom's idea. "He's taken with her."

"Just as she is with him."

"I should rip him apart for kissing her, but I'm not angry. Why's that?"

"You know." Dom gave him a knowing look, and he swore.

"I just... Logan and Jesse have been pack for years. It's not going to feel right without them. And don't get me started on Kate. I always knew Diana would be the one to leave first. While I'm still not sure I approve of Morely, it's obvious Diana's *guer* wants him."

He didn't know why he hadn't seen Kate's desire before. He'd always considered her his little sister, the weaker of the two females who needed defending. Logan and Jesse had always been the ones to protect her when he couldn't. But maybe that's because they'd sensed their tie even then. Though Dom swore the pair had no idea Kate wanted them as mates, Eric wondered if they'd deliberately skirted her feelings, not comfortable with the idea.

"Where's Kate now?"

Dom smirked. "After attacking the idiots on Monday, she's been sulking in the forest. She's finally coming to grips with being an adult. She knows it's time she claimed someone."

"Took her long enough." Eric shook his head.

Kate was nearly twenty-five years old, a ripe female who had to be nearing her first heat. She'd likely take a full pack, probably four or five males, to mate. Most of the adult females had mated, though some were still choosing the rest of their packs slowly. The unclaimed males in the clan liked to play as long as they could, and drifting from female to female, and male to male, gave them time to explore physical and emotional chemistry among their kind.

Like Malcolm. He was a terrific warrior. Strong, loyal, enduring. But he had yet to commit himself to any pack, and not for lack of attention. Several females had clamored to add him to their families, but Dom had insisted Malcolm remain unclaimed. As his guard, Dom had the ultimate authority on clan relations, aside from Eric. And since Eric spent most of his time working on Voider issues as related to Ravagers in general, he left clan politics to Dom. Now, however, he wondered why Dom had been so determined to leave Malcolm free.

"You *know* something, don't you?" he asked. "About Malcolm."

Dom shrugged. "Maybe."

Eric gritted his teeth. "Just once, it would be nice if you'd answer me when I ask you a question."

"I did."

"'Maybe' is not an answer."

Dom grinned. "Actually, it is."

Eric growled. Dom lost his grin and growled back. Anticipating the fight he richly deserved, Eric shoved Dom into the hallway.

"Downstairs, now."

Dom showed his teeth, a direct challenge Eric couldn't refuse. Pleased and needing some respite from the woman who wouldn't leave his mind, Eric prodded his guard's temper and picked up quite a following as they entered the large room downstairs reserved for group pleasure.

Two small packs engaged in sex continued to fuck when they entered. But Eric didn't care. His guard had a habit of forgetting his place. Time to remind him where he belonged.

"Come on, Prime," Dom rasped. "This isn't necessary." But the excitement on his face, the eagerness in his body as he tensed for battle, said otherwise.

Eric felt like an ass for ignoring Dom for three long days. Eric had needed the alone time with Vicki, and Dom understood, gladly giving him the space. But touch meant everything to Ravagers. Dom needed this as much as he did.

As he and Dom stripped out of their clothing, Eric wondered what Vicki would think if she saw this. Though he and the others had fucked her together, they often engaged in sex with each other because they needed it. The way he now needed Dom.

"Try to put up a good fight," Eric taunted Dom. "It's embarrassing to kick my guard's ass so easily."

Laughter floated around them. Dom hissed his annoyance, but his thick cock clearly showed how much he looked forward to their altercation.

"Prime, you're so lost in that female it's a wonder you haven't grown your own pussy. Are you sure you're up for a fight?"

Everyone in the room stopped to watch their prime and his guard throw down. A real treat, by Ravager standards.

"I'm going to ream you so hard, Dom." Eric's skin rippled as he shifted into his *guer*.

Dom did the same. Both kept their claws short, not wanting to hurt the other overmuch. Dom struck first, hard and fast. A true joy to watch in battle, he had half the crowd cheering for him. The other half urged Eric to take him slow, to work him over and feed the growing lust in the room.

Eric chuckled when Dom tried to rush him and tripped over Eric's foot. A shove to Dom's back enraged him into making another wrong move. They grappled with one another, and as they did, the press of their cocks grew rougher and more arousing. The tension between them heightened everyone's need.

Spectators began doing more than cheering. Several of the males initiated their own rough play. The heightened sexual awareness pulsed and throbbed, wrapping around Eric like a vise.

"That's it, guard. Try to take what you want. You want to fuck me, Dom? Want to shove that monster cock up my ass?"

"Yeah." Dom's voice wasn't much more than a hoarse rasp. "So hard, right now."

"Mmm. I'll bet you're wet too." Because Ravagers were sexual creatures, their bodies naturally lubricated themselves for sex. Females grew wet, as did males, but in their ass.

"Enough play. On your knees," Eric ordered Dom.

Dom roared back, "Make me."

The challenge delighted him. After some careful maneuvering, which had his cock positioned at Dom's ass, Eric put his guard in a chokehold.

As Dom lost his ability to breathe, Eric pressed harder. "Now you're mine."

Dom nodded and Eric let him go.

"Make it wet, first," he said, holding himself.

On a groan, Dom turned and took Eric's cock to the back of his throat. Excited and more than ready to spend, it took willpower not to explode in Dom's talented mouth, especially while the others watched.

He withdrew before he lost control. "Up against the table. Lean over it, but not too close. I want everyone to watch me take you."

Dom stood, drugged on lust, loyalty and need. Eric could feel his every emotion pulsing within him, tied to Dom by more than bonds of affection, but by the powerful energy of their entwined *guer*. Not every prime's guard could see what his prime needed, but Dom was special. His entire lineage had the ability to foresee their mates. He and Eric had been together since Eric had saved him from Nev and Nev's fucked-up family. They'd spent nearly all their lives together, and they'd stay that way until they died.

Complete with this Ravager he called his own, Eric took great delight in bending Dom over. He spread Dom's ass cheeks and licked his lips. "You're mine. All mine," he declared as he speared Dom with a rough thrust. Even with Dom's slick passage, the fit was tight. So much heat surrounding Eric's cock. So fucking good.

He moaned as he rode Dom hard, caught in the middle of the room with Ravagers fucking on all sides. Clan, pack, Ravagers touching and brushing against him, against Dom. The familiar bonds of ecstasy and fondness pushed him into a crashing orgasm sooner than he'd have liked.

He felt Dom come when he did and wrapped a hand around Dom's hot cock.

"Yeah, more," Dom moaned as Eric shuddered inside him. "Milk it, please."

Eric gripped Dom tight and caught the small bursts of cum still jetting from his slit. The pulse started an answering tide from his own sex, and he swore as the rapture of a second, smaller orgasm filled him.

The true sign of destined mates — the ability to experience each other's desires and build upon them. Something he'd never felt a need to share with Logan, Jesse or the girls.

As Eric stood there, embedded inside Dom, he felt a rush of emotion so intense it nearly blinded him. The sight of his clan loving one another, joining in bonds of warmth that only made them stronger, filled him with a sense of wonder. He could only hope to share this with Vicki someday.

"And with Malcolm," Dom added quietly, breathing hard. "He's pack, Prime. You'll see."

Eric swore with little heat, too winded from their joining, and withdrew from Dom. "I hate when you read me."

"I can only read you after mind-warping sex," Dom muttered and straightened. His cock was still half hard. "Fuck, Eric. That was so good."

"And so necessary." Eric stepped forward and took Dom in his arms. "I'm sorry I've been distant." He rubbed his cheek against Dom's, spreading his scent. Then he kissed his guard, his best friend, his lover. "It won't happen again."

"I know." Dom nipped his lip before stepping back. "You know, I smell like her too, now. It's subtle, but it's there. She's started her pack."

Dom grinned, and Eric swore. A few Ravagers near them sniffed and gazed curiously at their leader.

"You need to announce it soon," Dom reminded him. "Having Malcolm subtly run her by members of the clan, to spread the news without spreading the news, well, it's a clever idea to see who's tolerant and who's not. But you have to tell them outright at some point."

"I will. It's just…"

"I know. But it's easier to earn forgiveness than permission."

Eric scowled. "I don't need permission. I'm the prime."

"Exactly. Now I'm going to clean up. I suggest you do the same unless you want to meet with Walker and Chen smelling like Ravager cum."

"So wise, aren't you, my guard?" Eric grazed the Ravagers he passed, touching and stroking with acceptance.

"Always, Prime. I live to serve."

Chapter Ten

"So you're telling me Ravagers have sex all the time," Vicki said as she and Malcolm walked the grounds. To her surprise, Malcolm was giving her some valuable information. Though he still looked at her like the Big Bad Wolf wanting to eat up Little Red Riding Hood, he could carry a conversation.

"It's in our nature." He shrugged and kicked at a rock with his bare feet. "It's a basic need, one we don't think about all that much. To humans, it seems like a big deal." He paused, as if not sure how to address the issue of "humans" with the human.

"Don't worry, Malcolm. I know I'm not a Ravager."

"Which is what makes you so special."

"How's that?"

They crossed a stream. A few Ravagers in their *guer* raced by, sleek forms caught between man and what looked like wolf. What should have been awkward looked graceful. The long-limbed Ravagers moved through the woods as if they owned it. But she noticed the startled looks they shot her as they passed.

Malcolm answered her question. "I don't know if you've noticed, but other than your cousin, you're the only human—excuse me, Conduit—here."

"But I saw a bunch of human women with Ravagers in that bar where Eric found me." *Did I ever.* She blushed, and Malcolm grinned.

"I bet you did. Ravagers like sex; we're built that way. Women from other classes, both Voider and human, interest us. In fact, a bunch of the Savages living in the city have packs with non-Ravager females."

"Why? What's wrong with your own women?"

"Beside the fact they're so few?" he asked dryly. "It's an honor for a Ravager female to select her mates. We unclaimed males revel in feminine worship."

"Worship?" Vicki had a hard time understanding Ravager nuances. "Sounds like she's the one in charge if she's selecting you."

"She is," Malcolm said with an almost wondrous voice, his oddly intent stare giving her strange ideas. She swore she heard him say, "*You are.*"

"Our females were given to us by the great *guer* that lives in all things. She's more wild, beautiful and dangerous than any other creature we know."

His awe made her feel almost jealous. Had a man ever talked about her as if she mattered that much to him?

Malcolm's energy drew her closer. "You, Vicki, have a *guer* just as potent, just as wild, yet different. It's what's drawn the prime and the others. Not one male in all the clan would say no to you, if you asked them."

"No to what?" At his look, she blushed and felt stupid for feeling embarrassed. "Come on, Malcolm. I'm human. I don't belong here."

"I didn't think so, at first. Now…"

"Now what?" She tensed when he leaned forward to sniff her.

He closed his eyes and inhaled. "Your scent is sublime."

"I didn't know guys used that word."

He grinned, showing fangs, and she backed up a pace. "I'm well-read. And unclaimed, in case you were wondering."

"Ah, Malcolm? You're looking a little wild around the eyes." And hard as a rock. She couldn't help noticing the erection growing behind the swell of his jeans.

"It's you, Vicki. Dom told me to—" He stopped and looked behind her. In the space of a heartbeat, he turned from amorous to deadly. He tore off his shirt and simply grew, his jeans hugging his powerfully transformed *guer*. Now a large, powerful wolfman, he growled a warning. "Stay behind me."

A real threat in Eric's own woods? She didn't know if Malcolm thought to impress her with his *guer* or if she really needed to worry for her safety. And then she saw them.

Malevolent eyes glared at her through the trees. She could feel an oppressive weight of negative energy filling the area. Malcolm loosed a loud howl and raised his fingers, which turned into even longer talons as she watched. Stronger and thicker, his nails looked positively lethal as they turned from white to gray.

"When I tell you to, run," he snarled.

Three Ravagers attacked at once.

"Run!"

Definitely the Lawless clan. Vicki would never confuse the two again. In his *guer*, Malcolm looked vicious but healthy. A true predator ready to take on all comers. The intruders looked sickly, dirty, their matted fur sporting a dreadful smell, as if their darkness of soul had a stench.

Vicki had no intention of leaving Malcolm alone. She imagined help would soon be on its way. They'd passed others out here. But until help arrived, Malcolm was stuck with her.

She latched on to the negative energy of the Ravagers attacking Malcolm and tried to use it to bolster his strength, not sure if she could since they didn't touch.

The weaker males whined as Malcolm tore through them with ease. Another crept out of the shadowed woods and tried to take him by surprise. Vicki intervened by stepping forward. She grabbed a stick off the ground and prayed it was heftier than it felt.

She swung, hit, and freed one hand to latch on to the creature's arm. Ripping the Ravager's energy away, she used it to enhance her speed and let go of him. As in her fight with Mei Lin, the longer Vicki battled the Ravager, the easier it became to predict his moves.

She sparred with him, the deadwood in her hands granting her decent protection from the claws and teeth of her opponent. Until another Ravager blindsided her.

He knocked into her side, pushing her away from Malcolm and the Ravager she'd been beating.

Malcolm roared and turned to face this new threat when two more enemies appeared, looming over her.

"Do you smell that?" one growled to the other.

They dropped the English and spoke in barks and grunts and growls. She shouldn't have been able to understand them, but somehow, she did.

"Claimed," they both snarled. "Perfect." The larger of the two ran a claw over her cheek and bared his teeth. He jabbed her throat with his nail and licked at the blood. Then he backed away and disappeared into the forest once more. The one with him leaned down, no doubt with ill intent.

Just then Logan and Jesse barreled into the Ravager bent on eating her. Kate appeared and dragged her back from the fray. "Come on," she said and literally carried Vicki over her furry shoulder back to the house, where a huge mass of Ravagers had gathered.

As Kate left her to go back for the others, it dawned on Vicki she shouldn't have been able to recognize Kate, Logan or Jesse in their *guer*. Yet she did.

The burning in that spot on her left breast surged, and she gasped as the pain overwhelmed her.

Then Eric was there with Dom.

"Easy, Vicki. It'll pass." Eric stroked her hair.

He picked her up and handed her to Dom. She felt like a suitcase dumped on a hapless bellboy, but this was far from anyone's idea of a vacation. *Well, maybe a sexual fantasy come to life, fraught with danger and intrigue.*

Eric disappeared before she could ask any questions.

"Tell me what happened," Dom said, still holding her.

"I can stand." She scowled, embarrassed to appear frail amidst so much strength.

He ignored her and hugged her tighter. Others gathered around, and as she explained what had befallen her and Malcolm, she sensed their building rage, as well as their growing confusion as they stared at her.

The pressing power energized her, and she started to feel their bloodlust as her own. The heat in her breast swelled, but this time, her connection to Eric overwhelmed all other thought. As if he tethered her to him by some mystical means, she needed to find him again. To be near him.

"Ask questions later, Dom. Right now, we have a fight to finish."

Without questioning the rightness of her actions, she ran back into the woods, heedless of Dom's protests. She ran faster and harder than she ever had before.

When she reached Eric and the others, several Lawless Ravagers littered the ground. Malcolm bled from several wounds but seemed none the worse for wear. Eric looked seriously pissed, more so when he spied her.

"Dom?" he barked over her shoulder.

She turned to see Dom grinning like a loon. "Sorry, Prime. She took off. I couldn't catch her."

Eric and the others stared at her in shock.

"What?" She heard herself growl and said fuck it. Hell, if they could, she could. "Now what the hell is going on?"

"Just what I'd like to know," Eric yelled and rammed a fist into a young tree, breaking it in half. "Attack my clan in my own home?" he roared. "Dom, take her back. The rest of you, clean up this shit. Malcolm, you come with me."

* * * * *

Kate stared at Eric, astounded. She'd never seen him so angry. He glanced at his human again, and his lips tightened.

She forced herself not to scowl. Only sheer perversity could account for helping Vicki when by rights, Kate should have left her to rot at the hands of the Lawless clan. But her *guer* refused to let Vicki remain unprotected. Probably had something to do with the fact Eric, that great jackass, had claimed her. Hell, she could smell it all over the female. Might as well have stamped a label on her forehead.

If that didn't start a clan riot, she didn't know what would. Had the world suddenly turned crazy? Diana, a precious female, wanted *a human* as a mate. Her sister would claim a few more Ravagers, but the human would be a problem, especially since he didn't seem amenable to committing to Diana any time soon.

After her brief battle with Logan and Jesse a few days ago, Kate had nearly given up her idea to claim them as mates. They still had the nerve to talk about Vicki, as if the woman's shit didn't stink. The fact she'd outraced Dom and had helped Malcolm against their enemy would no doubt only further her standing as the perfect woman.

Kate seethed. "Should have let her alone when I had the chance."

"Kate?"

She turned to see Logan and Jesse approaching. Neither looked happy to see her.

"What?"

Logan grabbed her by the shoulders and shook her like a rag doll. *"You could have been hurt.* What were you thinking?"

"What?" Her teeth rattled from the force of his hold.

Jesse seethed. "You little idiot. Didn't you see the other Lawless curs waiting in the woods? They were a heartbeat from taking you. Dammit, Kate. Enough."

"Huh?" She couldn't seem to find her wits.

"I'm talking to Eric about this," Logan muttered but wouldn't meet her eyes.

"Good idea."

Jesse dragged her with him through the woods. When she tried to get free, Logan pushed her from behind.

Baffled and overpowered, she had no choice but to go with them. When they arrived home, they took her to Eric's room, shoved her inside, slammed and *locked* the door.

Leaving her face-to-face with her arch nemesis. Victoria Fox.

"Well, hi." Vicki shoved a hand through her thick black hair, tangled with leaves. "Thanks for getting me out of there."

"Ah, sure." What did one say to the woman she wanted to hate, especially when said woman was being nice?

"So what did you do? They stuck me in here and ditched me. I thought they couldn't do that to females. From what Malcolm said, you guys rule the roost."

"I'm sorry?" Why could she not think today?

"Been a while since I've seen Jesse and Logan. I hope they were okay?" Vicki ended in a question.

"Fine." She hadn't seen them? "I thought you were friends with the guys."

Vicki flushed, and Kate wanted to bite her. "Ah, we met briefly, when Eric kidnapped me." She frowned. "So what's the deal with you and your sister? You marked Sean? Did either of you ask him what *he* wanted?"

Now the dumb woman went on the attack? Did she not realize Kate had not only saved her but could rip her throat out before she could say boo?

"I didn't mark Sean." *I want the two Ravagers you've sunk your unworthy hooks into!*

"You didn't?"

"No, I didn't."

"But I thought you had sex with him." She colored when she said it.

"I did. Sex isn't always about marking or mating. Sometimes it fulfills a need." *Stupid human.*

"Ah, but… Okay. So why did your sister mark him?"

"Who can say? Sometimes our *guer* guides us to where we need to be." *Which is the only thing preventing me from killing you right now.*

Vicki blinked at her. "Right. So you want to tell me why you hate my guts?"

Had she been so obvious? Maybe the growling had given her away.

"Look, Kate, I can see your *guer*, your energy, whatever you want to call it. It always goes dark when you're around me. So what the hell crawled up your ass and died?"

Unfortunately, Kate could see what Eric liked about the woman. She had a lot of fight in her, and nothing appealed more to a Ravager, especially one as strong as the prime, than confrontation. Vicki should have been scared. She should have been cowering when Kate spread her fingers wide and transformed her fingernails into claws.

Instead she feigned a yawn. "Yeah, long nails. I'm so not impressed."

"Are you stupid?"

"Are you?" Vicki snapped. "I didn't ask to be here. I've been trying to leave for days, but your prime won't let me. I have a life, you know. A job I was pretty good at. Family, friends," she grumbled, but she didn't sound so sure.

Still, Kate wondered. Perhaps Dom had the right of it. Vicki didn't act like a woman gloating over her triumphs. She seemed confused, unhappy and a trifle…uneasy?

"You don't like my pack?" Kate couldn't help the emphasis she placed on "my".

"You can keep them. Hell, that didn't sound right. I like the pack. Really, it's just… I'm from a world where women do what they want when they want. All this marking talk is just weird. I don't *belong* to anyone. Like I'm really a possession." She snorted.

"So you're not looking forward to another romp with Logan and Jesse?" At the woman's raised brow, Kate hurriedly added, "And Dom and Eric?"

Vicki looked away. "I like Eric and Dom just fine. But I'm not a Ravager. Humans, even Conduits, don't have marathon sex orgies."

Vicki's face was bright red, and Kate felt a moment's compassion—that quickly died when she recalled with whom Vicki had first shared her "marathon sex orgy".

"So what? You want out of here?" Kate asked cautiously.

"Yes, I do."

Kate thought about it. If Eric found out she'd helped his mate escape, he'd kill her. Literally. A mated Ravager would do anything to protect the future mother of his pups. Then again, she thought as she considered Vicki, the woman was human, not Ravager. There wouldn't be any pups.

"Look, give me a few days, and I'll help you leave."

The hope in Vicki's eyes disturbed Kate on some level. "Really?"

"Yeah, but you can't say anything to the others. I'll get in a lot of trouble if you do."

"No problem. My lips are sealed." Vicki's excitement was catching. Her eyes lit up like gold coins. "Mind if I ask why you're helping me?"

"No."

Vicki shrugged. "Suit yourself."

"Just…" *Let it go, Kate. Don't show the enemy your weak spots.*

"Just what?" Vicki asked softly and touched Kate's hand.

Kate felt a ripple over her *guer*, a need to share her most basic desire. At that moment, Vicki looked like the answer to all her problems. The Conduit's eyes grew brighter. "Just don't take Logan or Jesse with you when you go."

Vicki smiled in understanding. "Ah, I see. No problem."

"And no more kissing them. No more sex." Kate couldn't stop herself.

"Gotcha." Vicki paused. "Can you help Sean leave with me?"

"Diana is enamored. She genuinely loves your cousin. She won't part from him." Kate couldn't understand it. Sean Morely was human. What did her sister see in him? What did her packmates see in Vicki besides a beautiful, stubborn, sexy woman? She contained the urge to growl again.

"Crap." Vicki fell silent, and the glow in her eyes faded as she stepped back. "You know, I'm exhausted. Wake me up when the others return, would you?"

She fell into the bed and was asleep in seconds, leaving Kate confused, frustrated and strangely enough, relieved.

Perhaps there was something to the strange human lying on her prime's bed.

* * * * *

"You saw her?" Nev asked as he stroked the hair of the cur servicing him. He spread his legs wider and arched into the warm suction of a wet mouth.

"Mm-hmm." Will seemed fascinated by his new sex toy.

"And?"

"Eric definitely claimed her. His scent is all over her. He'll have to make the announcement soon. I don't know how he's kept it quiet, but there's no rumbling of the news in the pack yet."

"Interesting." Arousal flared as his new pet licked the underside of his shaft and nicked his glans. "Good boy. Again," he murmured as the male blew him like a pro.

"What do you want me to do now?" Will asked, breathless.

"The meeting with Chen went as expected?"

"Yeah. He said if we find his stupid ring, he'll slaughter as many Savages as we want. And he'll lead more Watchers to their door. Whatever you want, once he has that ring."

"Good. Chen shows his hand too easily." Too bad. Nev had thought more of the man, but an attachment to a physical object? Pathetic.

The cur between his feet sucked hard, and Nev distanced himself from everything but the ecstasy spiraling through him. He unloaded and groaned, clutching the dirty hair of the young male before him. An unseasoned warrior, but a tremendous cocksucker all the same.

Once spent, he rasped, "Enough. Go." He watched his cock fall from the cur's mouth before he scampered away. "Will, what did you think of Eric's human?"

"She tastes divine." Will laughed. "I caught a bit of her blood on my finger. Surprisingly sweet for a human. And her energy...addictive. She's sexy. Nice body, pretty face. Very powerful. She did something to help that prick Malcolm defeat one of our lower packs. He took out four or five men, I think."

"Pity on the loss but interesting. A Conduit who enhances Ravager power? Might be worth as much as a connection to Chen."

"Maybe."

"Let me know when Eric announces his mate to one and all. Before we take her, we need to see how the others react. I'm still hoping they gut him for it."

"Yes." Will continued to stare at him, his desire evident.

A rush of excitement stirred his arousal once more. Will was older than his new pet, and ten times as vicious. "You in the mood for a little more blood?" Nev asked, pleased that he was just as hard as he'd been before coming.

"Yes, Prime."

"Come here."

Chapter Eleven

಄

Eric had to do it. Dom was right. The time had come. He couldn't wait anymore to fix the problems in his pack. At least his meeting with Diana had gone better than planned. Though she insisted upon claiming Sean, as was her right as a Ravager female, she agreed to extend her pack by one, to allow the same number of Ravagers the opportunity to bond.

Kate refused to talk to him, no surprise there. Instead of forcing her to listen, he avoided unnecessary tears and dealt with her future mates. While he could sense Jesse's and Logan's conflict about leaving his pack, the pair couldn't hide their excitement over Kate. Some undercurrents he'd been missing of late, apparently.

Annoyed that Dom always seemed to know what *he* didn't, he also had a firm talk with Malcolm. Once again, Dom was right. Malcolm's *guer* suited his, and the charming Ravager had a definite thing for Vicki, as well as a building case of the hots for his guard and for himself as well.

Now all Eric had to do was conquer one small, inconsequential Conduit.

He snorted. Inconsequential. Ha.

"We going to do this or what?" Dom asked, his eyes gleaming. "You know a hunt is the best way to forge the ties we need. A public claiming won't do it. Word is spreading about the scent marker all over her. You really nailed her, didn't you?"

Eric glared.

Dom laughed. "Right. Look, the Ravagers who saw her in action respect her, but the few left who didn't need to see what she can really do. They'll feel better about her if they know how ferocious she really is. Then they'll tell their friends out in the city. Before you know it, human mate or not, you'll be ass-deep in congratulations. Maybe even diapers if all goes well. Of course, that's provided Vicki doesn't bolt when she realizes you claimed her…accidentally."

Eric swore. Dom seemed to be enjoying his dilemma way too much. "I'll seduce her. The woman's as hungry for it as I am." Which secretly thrilled him. "Hell, the last few times I had her, she was begging for it. For me."

"Okay."

"She was." Eric felt defensive. So Vicki hadn't exactly begged him until he'd given it all he had to seduce her. She tested him at every turn, and the hell of it was she got him hard by being so fucking stubborn.

"Give me 'til tomorrow to set it up. And Prime, make sure you include Malcolm in your hunt. No better time to introduce him as a new member of the pack," Dom said with a wicked grin. "I've been wanting a piece of him for a long time."

"Why do you wait until the last minute to tell me these things?"

"Timing had to be right. He's ours, Prime. Just like Vicki."

Eric sighed. "Just like Vicki, great. If Malcolm's anywhere near as difficult as Vicki, I'm not just going to fire your ass. I'm going to kick it from here to the Lawless territory."

* * * * *

Vicki had a bad feeling about Friday night's events. The entire clan—those in attendance at the Savage homestead, anyway—rallied in the large area behind the house bordered by the tree line. They whispered and pointed when they saw her. Some looked at her with respect, others with caution and a few with hostility. She wondered if they didn't want her around Ravager tradition or if she'd irritated one and all in some other way. Who the hell knew?

Sentries had been positioned throughout the woods in preparation for this thing everyone called a hunt. According to Dom, the hunt celebrated past Ravager tradition, when the Ravager males used to hunt for their females in the years when females were plentiful, before life and their society changed. Since Ravagers considered their females sacred, no one was ever harmed during a hunt, but the exciting predator to prey relationship reminded everyone where they'd come from.

A place not of this world, Vicki thought, uneasy. In Cross Step, where everyone was different, it was easy to forget that the majority of the town's citizens came from other worlds.

Movement around her alerted her to the fact that half the Ravagers had transformed into their *guers*, while others, like Eric's pack — her pack — remained in human form. Diana stood next to Sean. Neither looked at the other, but any time a male stepped too close to Diana, her cousin pushed him back with a welling of fierce energy.

Vicki blinked in astonishment, wondering just when Sean's possessive streak had formed. For days he'd been bitching about being marked. Now, it seemed, he'd staked his own claim on Diana.

Kate remained apart from the others. Jesse and Logan stood behind her, their attention on the dark-haired female. The cloud of lusty energy swelling around the threesome built and built, and those nearest the group shuffled around on distracted feet.

The anticipation in the air all around her told Vicki something big was about to happen. She had a bad feeling it had to do with her, since Malcolm and Dom refused to allow her to move two steps without bringing her right back to Eric. And that was another thing. Why the hell was Malcolm now so chummy with Eric and Dom? And why did he look at her as if she were a piece of fresh meat?

He caught her stare and winked before licking his lips.

An answering desire zinged through her, and she forced herself to look away, happy at least that only a select few of these Ravagers revved her engine. *This is no time to get hot for just any Voider with attitude, Victoria. No way. Not here.*

Eric raised a hand, and the noise around them ceased. "It's been way too long since we last had a hunt. I'm sorry to say issues among our clan and other Voiders throughout town have kept me preoccupied, but no longer. As many of you may have noticed, we have some new faces among us."

Someone shoved Sean forward, and he swore back at them. Diana rolled her eyes but couldn't hide a grin.

"Sean Morely. Diana's claimed mate," Eric said in a loud, challenging voice. "He's human, a Conduit, and if any of you have the balls to take him on, go for it."

Sean scowled like a thundercloud. The grumbling around them grew louder until two hulking Ravagers in their *guer* stepped forward.

"Diana, you choose a human over your own kind?" One of them sneered at Sean.

"And a puny human at that," another added, hovering over Sean by a foot.

Sean didn't blink as he absorbed their energy and used it to throw them both back on their asses, several feet away. Diana grinned with pride and didn't protest when Sean threw an arm around her shoulders and anchored her to him, daring anyone else to pick a fight.

Dom laughed. "As you can see, Diana's mate has skills. Don't underestimate him. Prime never would have allowed the match were it not plain to see the male can hold his own."

Several around them grunted. Sean narrowed his gaze on Eric but didn't comment.

"More news," Eric added. "Kate has declared her own pack."

Cheers and clapping buoyed Kate to step forward.

"Jesse and Logan are no longer part of my pack, though I'll always treasure what time we had together." Eric smiled at the trio. "It's a great honor Kate has given them. Honor her well," Eric warned them, "or you'll answer to me."

Logan and Jesse responded with a solemn nod. The joy that should have been there wasn't, and Vicki knew she wasn't the only person there wondering what the hell existed among the three of them besides desire.

Eric turned to her before looking back out at the crowd. "And for my big news." The area quieted. "I've taken Malcolm into the pack to be claimed. He's a fine warrior, as you all know. His initiation into the family will take place tonight, once Dom catches him."

Malcolm seemed startled by the announcement, but several in the crowd snickered and cheered. She could only imagine what Dom would do to him, which had her quivering with unanticipated lust. Who would have thought she'd be aroused by the thought of guy Ravagers getting it on?

The desire on Dom's face as he eyeballed Malcolm was plain to see.

As was the satisfaction on Eric's as he watched *her*. Oh hell, he wasn't finished.

"And now we come to a truly joyous occasion."

The anticipation in the crowd swelled. Vicki felt dizzy waiting for Eric to drop his bomb. She just knew it wouldn't be pretty.

It wasn't.

"Once I catch my new queen, you'll see why she's the one who'll bear my young."

Everyone froze. The murmurs turned into shouts, growls and howls.

Dom and Malcolm gave her wicked smiles. Sean swore, as did Logan and Jesse, which must have irritated Kate because she turned on her heel and left the area. The pair raced to follow her.

Vicki glared at Eric. Did he really think she'd accept his announcement without an argument? She opened her mouth to retort but paused when he proceeded to strip down to nothing. Anger and arousal merged, the way they normally did around him. He changed into his *guer*, and the rest of the unchanged Ravagers followed suit.

She backed up a step. "I don't think—" Vicki jumped when Eric made a grab for her. Acting on instinct, she pulled the crowd's energy and molded it into a force she could use. Thrusting her hands out, she used the gathered power at those closest to her. Setting off a small, invisible explosion, she knocked several Ravagers to the ground. Definitely time for her to go.

She shot into the woods, her heart in her throat, and wondered how best to avoid this mess snowballing into one giant SNAFU. Except a large part of her didn't want to escape. It wanted worthy males to catch her, to take her, to possess her, finally.

So not normal.

God in heaven. Just days ago, she'd made one wrong turn and ended up sitting at the wrong table in the wrong bar. From that Eric thought he could just keep her? So what if he'd been the best sex she'd ever had? That the idea of taking him and Dom together made her wet just thinking about it? *And Malcolm, don't forget him now that Jesse and Logan belong to Kate.* She hated to think she really was slut material, but she couldn't escape the notion that desire for so many men couldn't be right. Hell, before she'd met her Ravagers, she'd been celibate for nearly a year.

She wanted to blame her raging desires on being marked. Better that than to admit she wanted to sleep around with a bunch of hot Voiders—hot Voiders now covered in fur and sporting erections. *Dammit.* Several ran on either side of her, and she increased her pace. How the hell could they run with an erection? she wondered hysterically as she turned to dodge a Ravager reaching for her. What if whoever caught her was allowed to keep her, and the Ravagers who found her first weren't Eric or Dom or Malcolm?

Yanking another burst of energy from those closest to her, she slammed those in her periphery into a tree and ran faster. Using the reserves she'd tucked away, Vicki resonated power and nimbly raced over the ground, seeing through the scattered moonlight as if it were day.

She continued to move, losing more and more of her pursuers until she wanted to laugh at the sheer elation of her escape. Vicki couldn't believe being hunted down like a wild animal could feel so liberating. Yet here, in nature's embrace, she felt the call of freedom reaching out to her. To let go of her control and simply let the wind take her was joyous.

A little too joyous.

Caught up in the rapture of her flight, she failed to notice the solid form directly in front of her.

She ran smack into Eric, who rolled with her as he took the brunt of their fall. Before she could move, Dom was there. Claws and hands pulled at her clothing, yanking and tearing with brutal efficiency until she lay stark naked, pinned between Eric's and Dom's aroused frames.

They were both hard and hot, thicker and longer in this form. Despite the alien feel of their coarse fur against her skin, she wanted to fuck them more than she ever had.

"No!" She squirmed between them to get free, not wanting to surrender so easily.

"That's it. So good." Eric moaned and stood. His erection was enormous. "Never give in, do you?"

"Fuck you," Vicki rasped, barely able to voice her rebellion through the lust rolling through her. Her teeth felt too large in her mouth and her tongue stumbled over the threats she wanted to make. The press of males nearing made little sense as her body filled out, grew, and pricked her with new sensations.

"So fucking hot," someone said, someone familiar. But she couldn't see through the darkness. Then pain, her head splitting in two. And once again, she could see everything. Colors were sharper, scents keener, sounds precise.

Dozens of Ravagers surrounded her, growling and groaning with surprise, with lust and with excitement.

"My mate," Eric thundered as another Ravager moved too close for comfort. He flung the male into the darkness, and Vicki heard him land with a solid thump. But the overwhelming sensations coursing through her body made little sense next to the ravaging need for something more.

"Don't forget this one," Dom said as he threw Malcolm to the ground. Malcolm wore bite marks all over his neck and chest. He rose on unsteady legs, his cock thick, his balls tight and his belly shuddering as he stared with hunger at Eric. *At her.*

Eric smiled at Malcolm but quickly returned his attention to Vicki. "Come here, pet."

"Not your pet," she rasped in a deeper voice than she should have had.

Eric gripped his cock, pearling with cream. The sharp claws around such tender flesh aroused her to a fevered pitch. She took several steps closer, despite her intent to keep her distance. She took one more step, and he yanked her to him by the hair.

"Now, Dom." Turning her in his arms, he made her watch, like all the others, as Dom shoved Malcolm belly-up against a tree, spread his ankles, and fucked him hard. The straining groans, the forceful sex and slick sounds of entry and retreat, made her mouth water. Especially when she watched Malcolm strain against his own climax. His scent permeated the small clearing in which they all stood.

"See how Dom owns him?" Eric asked in a gravelly voice. "He's reaming our new packmate, tunneling through that fine ass to make way for me, later." Eric bit her neck and shoved a hand between her thighs. He groaned as he played with her wet slit. "You're so sexy, so fuckable. *So mine.*"

He raised his hand from her pussy to his mouth and sucked his finger clean. Then he turned her around and kissed her until she couldn't think, could only feel.

The sounds of Dom and then Malcolm yelling out their pleasure resonated, but Eric dominated her attention.

He tasted like perfection, and she wanted more. Before she knew it, she was sliding down his body to take his fat cock in her mouth.

He groaned as he shoved forward, making her take him to the back of her throat, which should have been much more difficult than it was. A hazy state of consciousness took over as she accepted a small burst of her prime's seed. And then hands touched her, everywhere. Down her back, between her legs, over her breasts, her belly, her clit. Stroking and playing, teasing her into sucking harder, taking more and more of Eric until she felt as if she drowned in him.

"Yes," Eric hissed as he gripped her head by the roots of her hair and fucked her mouth until he came. Spurts of cum washed down her throat while her prime took his pleasure.

He finished and withdrew. Yanking her to her feet, he carried her in his arms past the throng of well-wishers back to the house.

The next thing she knew, she was blinking up at the human forms of Eric, Dominic and Malcolm. She lay in Eric's huge bed. Seeing the three of them, she suddenly understood why the bed had been built on such a grand scale.

"Now it's time to take care of you," Dom said with a sinful smile.

"Oh yeah," Malcolm agreed, his voice hoarse.

"You're ours now, Vicki. My mate, my queen. Part of our pack."

Dom chuckled. "You fully turned Ravager, honey. I've never seen that before in my life. You're the one."

"What one?" Lethargy and a sense she wanted more from these men robbed her ability to reason. With a lazy motion of her hand, she beckoned Malcolm forward and spread her legs wider. *Mine, all mine. I claim you three, forever.* Something inside her roared with satisfaction at the thought.

Enthralled with her wet pussy, Malcolm didn't ask what she wanted. He clamped his lips around her clit and gave her the pleasure she desired.

Dom leaned forward and caught her breasts in his hands, then his mouth. Teasing and playing, he and Malcolm brought her to the edge of orgasm in moments. But it was Eric she watched, gauging his reaction.

His narrowed gaze and shallow breaths brought her attention to his cock, once again erect and straining. "You want this inside you. But this time I'm taking what else belongs to me," he growled.

Before she could ask what he meant, Malcolm shoved a finger inside her and sucked harder on her clit. She arched up in climax, unable to stave the explosion taking her past reason. As she came down from the ecstasy, Eric repositioned her facedown on the bed while Dom and Malcolm left.

She wondered if he meant to initiate her in some private manner when Dom and Malcolm returned, wiping down their cocks, their concentration on her mouth. Understanding dawned, and she found her desire building once more.

She licked her lips. "You want me to—"

"Yes. You'll swallow them both. Eager to suck some cock, pet?" Eric breathed as he blanketed her body, prodded her thighs apart and shoved deep into her pussy. He pounded into her with enough force to touch the sweet spot deep inside her sex, but before he touched off yet another incredible orgasm, he withdrew.

She turned her head to see Eric suck his finger. Then he prodded her anus. "You made my cock nice and wet. But let's get you all ready for me." He slowly inched his finger inside her, and when it felt too much, he pulled out, spat on the digit, and pushed it in again.

"Eric," she breathed. God, the burn felt so incredibly good. The small bursts of pain were drenched by the pleasure of his touch. He added another finger and scissored them both, trying to make room for something bigger.

"Oh," she moaned, even as she instinctively rocked back to welcome his touch.

"Oh yes," Eric whispered as he withdrew his finger and prodded her hole with his cock. He moved past her tight rim, slowly but steadily, and the pain of his intrusion as he breached her was nothing next to the fullness of his possession. He continued to push until he finally seated himself all the way inside her.

Then he stopped, letting her feel all of him.

Dom sat down in front of her and moved until he could pillow her head with his groin. "Now suck me, Vicki. Blow me the way you did before. Trust me, my cum will make Eric's taking your ass so much better."

"As if it could get better," Eric teased, then groaned as Vicki tensed around him. "Easy. I don't want to hurt you."

"You already hurt me," she argued but couldn't help the tantalizing sight of Dom's arousal right in front of her. It didn't make sense that she should want him. She'd never been one for swallowing either, yet she wanted another taste. Something about their seed was addicting. But she'd dwell on that later. Much later. A glance next to her showed Malcolm jerking off as he watched the threesome.

"No, Malcolm. Don't lose it, not unless you're inside a warm mouth, pussy or ass," Eric ordered, his tone lazy but approving as he spoke to their newest packmate.

"Yes, Prime," Malcolm said on a moan. "But it smells like sex in here, and I'm so fucking hard."

"Ah, yes." Eric pumped slowly, then harder as Vicki took Dom in her mouth. She sucked and licked, took his balls in her hand and rolled them gently, pleased when he hardened to the point where she knew he'd soon blow.

"Fuck, oh, Vicki," Dom sighed. "My queen, yes, *yes*." He shook as he spilled inside her mouth.

He came in a steady rush as she fondled him, enthralled by the strength and scope of his need. Vicki could feel his desire, not just for the group, but for her, and his affection resounded in every fiber of her being.

Eric rode her, the burn a pleasure in itself. "That's so good, honey. You gave it back, all the pleasure. Now it's Malcolm who needs you. Show him how good it can feel."

She couldn't deny him, even if she'd wanted to. Turning her head, she watched the Ravager approach. Handsome, tall and so damn hard he looked in pain, Malcolm moved to join her but was intercepted by Dom.

"Dom," Eric rasped and quickened his pace. "I can't last much longer."

"Just a taste."

Arousal throbbed through her body as she watched Dom go down on his knees and take Malcolm into his mouth. The sight of such a strong male sucking off another made her moan with need.

Malcolm tilted his head back, the strong cords of his throat exposed as Dom pleasured him.

"Enough," Eric growled and slammed inside her. "Let's finish this before I explode."

She wiggled her hips, and he slapped her ass.

And then Malcolm was there, taking Dom's place. Longer but not as thick, he posed a challenge just to fit him inside her mouth. She took him with no problem. Unable to question her abilities surrounded by so much carnal need, she rode the wave.

She bobbed over Malcolm and moaned when Dom joined them and rubbed her clit. Eric pounded into her, harder and harder as Dom murmured something she couldn't make out. Malcolm stroked her cheeks as she breathed him in, impossibly thick and on the verge of coming.

"Please, Prime. I'm there, so ready," Malcolm moaned.

"Come hard. Let her swallow all of you," Eric growled and slammed one more time inside her before stilling, just as Malcolm jetted inside her mouth.

Dom pinched her clit, and the rapturous energy filling the room drove her into an orgasm so intense she could feel everyone in the room with her. Dom, Malcolm, Eric and she were one body, one source of joy as the throbbing pulse of unity tied them together in a way she couldn't explain. She just knew everything was different.

Too exhausted be afraid, she felt them leaving her, only to return to clean their seed from her. Eric brought her a glass of water and stroked her hair as she drank, but it wasn't enough to take the taste of her mates from her.

She didn't want to forget.

"For such a pain in the ass, you turn me inside out, you know that?" Eric said in a low, soothing voice.

Dom chuckled. "So romantic."

"Geez, Prime. Even I can do better than that," Malcolm joined them. His words cracked on a yawn.

Vicki wasn't the only one exhausted.

"Tomorrow, Malcolm, I'll get a taste of you," Eric purred.

"Hell." Malcolm couldn't hide the excitement from his voice.

"Welcome to the pack. Now lay your ass down and go to sleep." Eric tucked Vicki between him and Dom, and she felt Malcolm's hand on her flank as well.

Four grown people sharing a bed. She thought of wolves in a pack sleeping together and smiled. Her last thought before sleep claimed her.

Chapter Twelve

Vicki woke the next morning in a tangle of arms and legs. Before she could protest, Eric turned her onto her back and thrust deep. He took her quickly, while the others watched and rubbed all over one another. She came at the same time Dom, or Malcolm, hell, maybe both did. Eric followed shortly after, shuddering as he filled her.

"You're supposed to soothe the need, but I'm getting hungrier for you every second you're mine," Eric admitted. He kissed her hard then withdrew and rolled off the bed. "Time for some damage control this morning."

Dom stretched beside her. "Damage control? You mean, to explain how a Conduit, a non-Ravager like Vicki, turned feral yesterday during the hunt?"

"Vicki, you were beautiful," Malcolm added, his voice husky. "I've never seen a Ravager female who wasn't dark, with the exception of Dom. I mean, you were, but your eyes were so bright. Like the fucking sun."

"Now that's poetic. The fucking sun. Nice." Dom elbowed him in the gut, leaving a laughing Malcolm there to hug Vicki until her hormones started singing again.

I am so not normal. Voider porn, here I come.

"Malcolm," Eric warned.

Malcolm darted off the bed.

Vicki blinked as she suddenly lay all alone. The past days' confusion set in, and she realized she'd become a Ravager play toy. Make that, sex toy. Her cheeks burned with embarrassment—and a strange sense of pleasure.

"Hold on one minute, all of you." She sat up in bed, conscious of her nudity when all three men stared at her breasts. Swearing, she found a sheet and covered herself. "Explain what the hell happened last night."

"Besides the sex?" Malcolm looked confused.

"Besides the orgy, you mean," she snapped. "Yesterday was beyond weird." She stared in horror as what Eric had said penetrated. "You talked about me being a queen and bearing your young! *Shit, shit, shit.* I've had shots, but you guys can impregnate anything, can't you?"

Dom tried to stifle a grin, and she threw a pillow at him.

"It's not funny."

"Hold on, Vicki." Eric sighed. She thought she heard him mutter about her being a stubborn, sexy woman, but his frown took her aback. "You don't want kids?"

"Ah, yeah, eventually. But geez, Eric. It hasn't even been a week since you carted me off to Ravager funland."

He raised a brow. "Funland, eh? What's the problem? You don't like fun? Was the sex not to your liking?"

She flushed. "I'm not going to pretend I didn't enjoy it. You guys know what you're doing."

He frowned. "You *guys*?"

"Oh hell. You're a king in bed. A stud between the sheets. You make me wet by simply breathing. Happy now?"

"Actually, yes." He grinned, and she wanted to slap his handsome face because she wanted him *again*.

"My point, your humbleness, is that I barely know you. We fucked. Yeah. And I screwed around with Dom and Logan and Jesse too. And let's not forget Malcolm," she added when he opened his mouth.

"Let's not," he muttered.

"Good sex—"

"Great sex," Dom countered.

"Does not lead to marriage, not if you're human." She glared at the three of them.

"But you're not human, you're a Conduit. And you're mine. My mate, my queen," Eric said, a bite to his tone.

He had a problem? She'd give him something to chew on. "Well, good, wolfie, because as Mrs. Prime, I demand you let me off this goddamn compound."

Dom crossed his arms and smiled. "I was so looking forward to this."

"And you, shut it!" she growled at him. "You're as much to blame as he is. You picked me in the first place."

Dom glanced knowingly at Eric, who sighed and said, "You were right. *Again.*"

Malcolm rolled his eyes. "Dom's always right. Your guard knows everything you need before you need it, Prime. He's a legend…in his own mind," he added with a chuckle that had Dom frowning at him.

"Funny. Look, you're pack now. Call him Eric," Dom suggested.

"Eric," Malcolm repeated. "He's as much a marvel as you are, or at least, he was, until you pulled probably the only woman in the world who could bear your—" he paused at the glare Vicki shot him. "Ah, I mean, no way anyone could have turned a human feral the way you did, not unless you had a shitload of power, which you obviously do." He snickered. "Nev Lawless is going to hate this."

Eric nodded and sobered. "Dom, increase the watch. Vicki—"

"Don't *Vicki* me." On the one hand, she could feel his pleasure, that he had her, not just some woman he'd supposedly turned feral, whatever that meant. But on the other, he hadn't heard a word she'd said. With a snap of her hand, she twisted his energy around him and pulled him closer to her.

He glared. "Cut that out."

Malcolm's eyes widened. "Holy shit. I thought Dom said she had to touch you to do that."

He was right, but Vicki couldn't think about the strange turn her ability was taking.

"Don't piss me off, or I'll do it to you too," she warned. "Now look. If you expect me to stay here, you'd better start thinking flowers and candlelight. I want to see my family whenever the hell I want to, and I plan on continuing to work with Sean for S&V Retrievals. We spent years building up that company, and we're good at what we do. You want me to stay, I'll need an office I can work from when I'm here. Deal?"

She expected Eric to scoff at her lengthy list, especially the part about her continuing to work with Sean. Vicki kept the disappointment at bay. *So what that I've become so used to them while I've been here? This is just a fling. I barely know them.* A few weeks at home, living a passionless existence filled with Voider trouble, would be just the thing.

Eric smiled, showing sharp teeth. He kissed her smack on the lips. "Deal. Dom, Malcolm, she's yours. I have a meeting with Walker and…someone important later."

He left for the bathroom before she could respond. She heard the shower running.

"Deal? What does 'deal' mean?"

Dom laughed and swung her up in his arms. He kissed her then nuzzled her breast, where the burning mark now throbbed with a pleasant hum, a beacon of energy she clearly felt as Ravager. "It means you're part of the family. Our mate—our *wife*—for those of us who think like a human." He wiggled his brows. "How great is this?"

Wife? A large ball of emotion clouded her thinking, and for a moment, she felt pure delight in belonging with her new pack. Until she reminded herself she was a regular woman who shouldn't take pleasure in marathon orgies. Fox and Morely women were much more circumspect with their lovers, er, husbands, as in, one "mate" at a time. Good Lord, what would Gran say? Hell, what would Gran do to these guys if she didn't approve?

Malcolm rubbed her shoulder and slapped Dom on the back. The Ravager had tears in his eyes, and that quickly her worry faded under concern for Malcolm. "I've been on the outside looking in for a long time. Now I've not only got a pack but a female as well. It doesn't seem real."

His wonder and distress tugged at her. Dom put her down and hugged Malcolm. To her shock, he swept Malcolm into a steamy embrace that had both men groaning.

"It's real, all right," Dom said on a sigh. "And if I didn't have a shitload to do, I'd get you off right now. But with Eric handling outside clan matters, I've got to do a few things in-house. Malcolm, stay with our new queen. Okay?"

Malcolm turned glittering eyes her way. "My pleasure."

Dom turned to the bathroom but stopped and pointed at Malcolm. "For your sake, don't forget what we talked about. I'd hate for Eric to rip you open and gut you before we can see where this family takes us."

Malcolm groaned. "It'll be hard, but I won't disrespect my prime."

"Your packmate," Dom said with a smile.

"Yeah. Packmate." Malcolm lit up, and Vicki had to smile. The leer he gave her, however, wiped the grin from her face. Damn, Malcolm was hot. "Anywhere else, right?"

"You got it." Dom disappeared into the bathroom and shut the door.

Malcolm turned to her. In two steps he took her in his arms and kissed her. Like magic, he melted her resistance with those firm, warm lips.

"Malcolm, what—"

"Later, mate. First I need to ease your need. You smell so sweet." He licked his way down her body, and when he burrowed between her thighs, she stopped all thought. Her questions could wait. For now.

* * * * *

Later that evening, Vicki sat with Malcolm at the end of one of the long tables in the expansive dining room. Dozens of other Ravagers smiled her way when they entered but gave her and Malcolm privacy all the same.

"They like me now?" she asked as she dug into the meatloaf Rule had prepared. "A few days ago I was someone to be tolerated or ignored. Yesterday, half of them seemed to hate me."

"They love you now," he said with satisfaction. "You really don't understand what happened, do you?"

"Hello, genius. I've been with you Ravagers for a week as of today. Sue me if I'm not up to date on what's what around here."

He grinned. "You have a smart mouth. Good thing it's so talented at other things," he ended in a whisper, focused on her lips.

She colored, hoping he didn't scent her desire with those hellishly keen Ravager senses. "Tell me what I don't understand."

They'd spent a surprisingly pleasant day together. Eric had checked on her once when he'd returned from town doing God knows what. She'd seen Dom on and off all day. Mostly he'd been beefing up security. Thanks to the attack the other day, the Savages kept on full alert. Malcolm had proven to be charming, attentive and a font of knowledge.

"Like I told you before, not all Ravagers can impregnate a female. The *guer* of both male and female has to be in total alignment."

She nodded. "It's not about her being in heat, although that's a part of it. It's more about their energy bonding accordingly." Vicki knew about energy. She lived to manipulate it, so she understood most of what he was saying.

"Right. Her heat just places her *guer* in a more manageable state to accept not only the male's seed but his life force. It's the perfect union of spirit and body. What you don't understand is that Eric's *guer* is one of the most powerful Ravager spirits we've ever seen in this world. That's why everyone accepts his leadership. Ravagers respect strength. And Eric is beyond normal. He's Prime." Malcolm's pride was unmistakable.

To her amusement, she felt it as well. As if Eric's conceit needed any help from her. "That I get." She took another bite of meatloaf, allowing Rule his own arrogance. The man could seriously cook.

"Eric pulled your *guer*. He tapped into your energy and brought it out of you, Vicki. You turned feral, meaning, you became a Ravager for that period of time in the woods." Malcolm's throaty voice and darkening eyes alerted her to his arousal. "You have no idea what it was like to be a part of that moment."

"Pack," she murmured and stroked his arm. She was growing to really like the touchy-feely Ravagers, taking comfort in their way of bestowing affection.

"Family." Malcolm nodded and caught her hand in his. But when he guided the other hand holding her fork to his lips and stole her food, she pulled back. He laughed. "You're rabid, aren't you?"

"I belong to the prime and his wacky pack. You tell me." *I belong. Oh shit, I've fallen in love with these louts.* She stuffed her face full of food before she did something stupid, like blurt her love out loud. She needed to think about this situation. Lord, did she.

Malcolm grinned. "Prime's pack is important, no doubt. It's odd that just as you arrive, the females the clan has been waiting for, forever it seems, finally do the right thing. Diana and Kate needed to be on their own years ago."

"I still don't understand why Eric didn't just cut the cord and force them to marry." Not that she wouldn't have argued if someone—Gran—tried to force her to marry. But still. These guys seemed pretty stoked about procreating.

"Force them? Force females?" He seemed stunned at the possibility, and she thought again about all she knew of Ravager relationships. Did females really rule their packs?

"Malcolm?"

Malcolm shifted in his seat, his discomfort more than interesting. "Oh look, there's Dom." He took off like a shot, leaving her alone at her end of the table.

No one else approached, but she saw the curious looks, the smothered grins. As much as Vicki wanted to be annoyed at being the center of attention, she found herself trying to integrate into her new clan. And how fucked up was that?

Sex was really all she knew about these people, she thought glumly. Gran would have a field day with her new friends. Alpha males, animalistic Voiders who had sex wherever they liked. Family units consisted of one woman and two or more males. Rarely did any of the females have children. Of those who lived in the city, there were a few more pregnancies, but not many. Oh and Vicki had been forbidden to leave without her husband's—make that husbands'—consent. Yeah, right. Gran would tear her a new one for even *thinking* about staying here.

So why did leaving make her want to cry?

Vicki felt safe here. She felt home, content...*loved*. Not one of her pack had said a thing about how they felt about her, but she could sense the caring. The energy around her alleged mates pulsed with arousal, excitement and adoration.

"Must be losing my freakin' mind." Because she felt it too, all that nice, messy *love*.

A body plunked down across from her. She looked up to see a male she didn't recognize.

"Ah, can I help you?"

He gave her a toothy grin. "Flowers, right?" He nodded at someone behind him, and a dozen or more bouquets appeared on her table, surrounding her with roses, irises, orchids and more.

"Thanks?" she said absently when he walked away.

"What the hell is all this?" Sean asked as he filled the seat the other Ravager had vacated. Diana sat next to him, and the pair looked surprisingly at peace.

"Who the hell are you and what have you done with my cousin?" Vicki asked him. She laughed when he flushed and looked askance at Diana.

"Come on. I haven't been that much of an asshole." At her silence, he blinked. "Have I?"

"That's my cue to leave," Diana murmured. "I'll go grab us some dinner. Nice flowers, Vicki." She left them alone.

"So what's your deal?" she asked her cousin, greedy to spend some time with her *other* family again.

"Oh hell." He groaned and clutched his head by his hair. "She's brainwashed me. I can't do anything without that woman's face popping into my head at all hours."

"Uh huh."

He lowered his voice. "And Vicki, she's...insatiable. It's like she can't get enough of me. And it's mutual. I'm no longer normal."

"As if you ever were. Do I really need to hear this?" Vicki contained her laughter at his pained expression.

"I'm serious. The other night, when you were being chased through the woods—and no, please do not give me any details. I've heard enough already."

She blushed.

"The other night I think I turned into one of them. It was totally weird. We were, like, intimate, and the world went cloudy. I felt furry, I swear."

"You turned feral." She explained what Malcolm had told her. "Eric was powerful enough to pull that from me, but I'm thinking Diana must be pretty strong to pull that from you."

"Yeah, or it could be because we're Conduits. I mean, we're 'out there' even as Conduits. We play with energy differently than others do. Might be why they were taken with us in the first place." He glanced around her. "So again, what's with the flowers?"

"I'm not sure."

At that moment, another group of Ravagers approached carrying candles of every shape, size and color. They placed them around the table, snickered and walked away.

Vicki suddenly understood.

"Candles too? How…romantic." Sean coughed to cover a laugh.

The table was littered with candles and flowers, a gluttonous display of overdone affection. It was so silly and so wonderful she had to blink not to cry. *Twice in one day with the tears, I'm going for a record.*

Vicki cleared her throat. "Shut it, Sean. Look, I think we have to deal with life here as a new reality."

"No, really?"

She would have belted him if the sarcasm hadn't been warranted. "Are you planning on leaving Diana any time soon?"

He stopped smiling. "No. You so eager to get back to town and deal with more retrieval work? Because earlier, Dom pointed me to a fully loaded room, the office of our dreams, and mentioned how we were free to work out of an office here, when we weren't in town doing business. As in, we will at some point leave this place and be Ravagers along with the rest of them. In our own unique way, of course."

"An office, here?" Good old Dom. Busy with clan business, my ass.

"Aside from what everyone else thinks, I feel it too, Vic. I can't explain it, but it's like we belong here now. Does that make sense to you? Or am I just totally a vegetable? The sex is frying my brain in a really, really good way."

She laughed. "Still gross, but I know exactly what you're saying." She leaned close. "Thing is, if you give in too easily, you'll lose face. They like a challenge."

"Hell, they're not much different from humans in that respect. Nothing worse than a woman catering to your every need," he had the audacity to say as Diana returned carrying his plate of food. He frowned when he saw Vicki glance from his plate to Diana and back. "Stop. She's just being nice because I threatened her earlier."

"Really?"

"Just mind your own business." Sean thanked Diana and stroked her cheek when she sat. The woman smiled at the open sign of affection, and more, of acceptance.

God, the woman really did love Sean. Their energy, their *guers*, as the Ravagers liked to think of them, merged without a seam.

Vicki sighed. "We're going to have to talk to Gran. Let the family know we're still alive."

"I've been on the phone with that woman daily," he grumbled. "She's invited us all over for Monday night dinner. Diana and me, and you and your *entire* pack. Talk about spreading the love." He snickered.

A glance over her shoulder showed her pack bearing down on her. Three Ravagers and her. She turned back to Diana. "Hey, Diana, I heard you're going to fill out your pack."

"Yes."

"More mates, right? But not another female, more males."

"No. There's just one female to a pack. And not all packs have a female, there are so few of us."

By the panicked expression on Sean's face, he realized where she was steering the conversation.

"So your mates, you'll all share each other equally, right? Because as I understand it, pack is pack. Family."

"Of course." Diana smiled and tucked into her plate laden with food.

"Don't say it," Sean warned, his face on fire.

"Sean, you'll have to get over your sexual hang-ups. Like I've been saying for years, it's not about gender, it's about the person inside." She couldn't *wait* to tease him about this. Fodder for years to come.

Diana frowned. "This is an issue? You didn't seem to mind Nathan earlier."

"TMI, honey, TMI." Sean rubbed his eyes and slid his hands through his hair in agitation.

Vicki tried not to laugh. But by the time Dom, Eric and Malcolm reached her, she had tears in her eyes as she tried to catch her breath.

"What's so funny?" Dom asked.

Vicki laughed harder at her cousin. "Remember when I asked you about the Ravagers sharing you among their females? Never thought I'd see them sharing you with the males."

"Shut up," Sean said in disgust. "Come on, Diana. Let's let Chuckles here share her candlelit dinner with her boyfriends. Oh and, Vicki? Gran really wants to meet them...*all*." The evil grin he shot her did wonders to cure her humor.

"Damn."

"Vicki?" Malcolm asked.

"Did you like the flowers and candlelight?" Eric asked, sounding pleased with himself.

She sighed. "We really need to talk."

*****

The three males of his pack, those who could think *logically*, sat together on the bed while Vicki paced in front of them trying to make a point he clearly wasn't getting.

Eric didn't understand. Even though Dom had tried to explain it to him, dating seemed like such a stupid concept. What exactly did Vicki need from him he hadn't already given her? After their time in the forest and last night, he was pretty damn sure he'd planted a seed that took root. His heart swam with delight at the thought.

His *guer* had welcomed her. He'd marked her, then claimed her—claimed *a human*—an unheard of event for a Ravager, let alone the actual prime. By accepting her as his queen, he'd made her the most important part of the clan, one they hadn't had in this world since before the Voids opened. God willing, she'd do what no female had done since leaving the homeworld—enhance the fertility of their species.

Vicki blathered on. "Eric, guys, we don't really know each other. The flowers and candlelight was a way of saying let's go out on a date."

He saw confusion on Malcolm's face as well. Good to know he wasn't the only one.

"Told you," Dom murmured. Mr. Right, yet again.

"Dick," Eric murmured back.

"Eric, listen to me," Vicki insisted. She scowled at him, and he wanted nothing more than to bend her over the desk and take her. Or maybe this time he'd have her sit on top of him, so he could fuck her pussy while Dom or Malcolm rode her ass. Or...

"Eric," she snapped. "Tone down the hormones for a minute. This is exactly what I'm talking about."

Malcolm licked his lips, his gaze vacillating between Eric's and Dom's erections and Vicki's mouth.

She sounded a little breathless when she continued. "And you too, Malcolm. I'm trying to tell you that as much as you want me to stay here, I don't think I can."

Eric, Dom and Malcolm froze.

"Living with someone is freaky enough. But it's like we got married, mated, whatever, and I barely know you. What's your favorite color?"

"Red," Eric said.

Dom answered, "Blue."

Malcolm shrugged. "Never really thought about it."

"Mine is yellow."

"Like your eyes," Dom said.

"My eyes are brown." Vicki glared, her eyes turning even more golden.

Wisely, Dom held his tongue.

"So you want to know everything about us, is that it?" Eric asked, trying to know why she couldn't stay with them. His *guer* wouldn't let her leave, and if he wasn't mistaken, she didn't really want to go.

"I should, don't you think?" she asked, obviously exasperated. She planted her hands on her hips and leaned forward, drawing attention to her luscious breasts.

"What I think is that you should help me claim Malcolm before we fuck so hard you have trouble walking tomorrow. That's what I think."

Arousal flared. He deliberately allowed his to seethe, to entangle her own.

"Eric, we need to—" she said in a husky voice before Malcolm's moan stopped her. "Oh hell. Get his clothes off and let's get to it."

Dom grinned and stripped. Eric and Vicki took their clothes off before moving to Malcolm. As one, they undressed him, touching him everywhere.

"God, you're so strong," Vicki breathed as she ran her hands over his ripped abs. "No body fat, I swear."

"Too bad you don't know what it feels like to ram a cock up that ass," Dom whispered as he leaned forward to bite the base of Malcolm's throat.

Malcolm sighed and clutched Vicki to his chest when she sucked on his nipples.

"Unfortunately, this won't take long," Eric said on a laugh, which turned into a groan when Malcolm opened his beautiful, brown eyes and stared at him with sexual hunger. "On your knees, mate," he said deliberately. "Dom and Vicki, and now you. You know, I never claimed Jesse and Logan. They were pack, but they weren't mine. But you are."

Malcolm panted, his cock slick from the pre-cum leaking from his slit, that same cream Vicki was rubbing all over his shaft. Dom shoved his fingers between Malcolm's ass cheeks and Malcolm cried out.

"He's wet. And ready."

Eric grinned. "Then let's not waste any more time." He forced Malcolm to his knees and held out his cock. "Suck it until I tell you to stop."

While Malcolm laved him with loving attention, Dom and Vicki stroked both Malcolm and Eric, building the tension among them into a frenzy. Eric nearly shot into Malcolm's mouth when Vicki rimmed his asshole with a small, delicate finger.

When she pinched his nipples, Eric hurriedly withdrew from Malcolm's hot mouth.

"Now, Malcolm. On your hands and knees. Open for me."

Malcolm groaned, shaky as he turned and waited.

Dom knelt by his side and reached under him. Pumping Malcolm's cock, he jerked off their new mate while Vicki kissed Malcolm everywhere she could reach. Eric knelt and shoved home in a one slick, hot push.

Malcolm came hard, crying out as he spurted over Dom's hands. Eric thrust twice more before joining him, coating Malcolm's rectum with seed, a scent of overpowering trust and desire as he let go of his *guer* to snap that final bond in place.

When he withdrew, it was to see Dom and Vicki welcoming Malcolm into the family, a family that had only recently acknowledged Vicki's place in the Ravager society. *Blessed beyond thought, that's what I am*, he thought as he shared the intense belonging he felt deep inside.

"Mine," he said of his pack, and lay down on the floor with them as they roused themselves to another wave of passion. The tighter the bonds, the tighter the union. Nothing would tear them asunder.

No matter who he had to kill to keep them safe.

Chapter Thirteen

On Monday night, Nev Lawless waited with Will and close to fifty hungry Ravagers, fanged and furred, outside the Morely house in the middle of town. Situated in a residential neighborhood where the houses didn't have much room amongst them, the building itself was large, an aging Victorian monstrosity that had seen better days. Oddly enough, the place felt empty.

"I don't know, Nev," Will said with a shrug. "I watched Eric and his fucked-up pack enter an hour ago. Diana was with them and that human bitch's cousin as well. But something's not right."

Not what he wanted to hear. Nev wanted to finally end this. If all went well, he'd have Eric's mate in the palm of his hand, his to torture while Eric watched. And Dom would be there. His heart raced at thoughts of seeing the golden Ravager again.

At least this plan had merit. Thanks to their informant, they knew Kate had all but disappeared from the Savage clan days ago. No one had seen her since, and Jesse and Logan, apparently Eric's *old* packmates, had vanished as well. So much for using any of them as bait.

He wondered how Malcolm fit into the picture. The shithead had done some damage to the Lawless clan in that last attack. A worthy adversary, at least. Should Nev allow him to live or not? Perhaps he'd give him to Will, if Will didn't have his hands full with Diana. No matter what Will said, Nev knew he wanted a pack. Because without a female, he had no chance at a future.

Speaking of their future…

"You sure the Salinas won't interfere?" Nev asked Will, just to be on the safe side.

"Chen's taking care of them. Listen to the surrounding silence. No one's around. The whole fucking neighborhood is practically empty."

Nev nodded. Thank the Void for that stupid ring. Chen would do anything to get it back.

"Fine. Have half of them surround the house. You, me and the other half will take out anyone not Ravager, except for Eric's bitch. I want him to watch while I play with her. Have them do their best not to outright kill Eric and the others. Not yet."

Will grinned and spread the word. The death squad readied to breach the entrance of the Morely estate. After a signal from one of his scouts, they entered in a rush.

No one in the front rooms or the upstairs. No one in the basement either, until he scented Dom near. Arousal stirred.

"Will?"

Will frowned. "Search for a hidden door. I can smell them."

"Me too," Nev growled, his hunger for Dom an agonizing need, one that almost overshadowed his desire for revenge on the Savage clan and Eric in particular.

They searched through bookshelves and along the cracked paint peeling over the walls. The basement was an odd, untended area compared to the rest of the finely furnished house.

And then something special happened. The wall split in front of him. No, not the wall, a hidden doorway groaned as it slid behind the cracked wall paneling.

They walked a few meters before a rush of air breezed by them. And suddenly, they weren't in a house anymore but standing on a football field illuminated by blazing lights. Blinking into confusion, Nev tried to figure out what the fuck he'd walked into. And where the hell had all his men gone? Only a dozen or so remained with him.

In the center of the field, an old lady waited with her hands on her hips. "Well, come on. We're waiting on you."

Ravagers, both Savage and Lawless, as well as a host of other Voider species, filled the overcrowded stands surrounding the field. There, in the front, sat Tommy Chen.

"What the fuck?"

Chen grinned and waved, wearing his trademark sunglasses.

Beyond caring about his own protection, Nev narrowed his focus on the party sitting right behind Chen. Dom sat between another Ravager and a pretty human female, who sat next to *Eric Savage*.

Nev stormed toward the group, his men in tow, and neared the old woman. She looked enough like Eric's female to be a relation. Obviously older, yet the woman stunk of power.

He stopped, suddenly unsure about this trap he seemed to have stepped into. One of Chen's making? But why would Chen ally himself with Eric and the woman who'd stolen his precious ring when he had a price on her head? Did Chen have the ability to transport people? Because Nev still didn't understand how he'd been in the Morely house one minute and in this school football stadium the next.

"Well, you're not totally stupid," the old lady muttered. "You're here because I teleported you. And in case you were wondering, the rest of your annoying pack is back in your woods, well away from my house." She dared turn her back on him and pointed to Eric. "You, Prime, come here."

Will tried to jump past Nev, eager to sink his teeth into anyone not deserving of the title.

To Nev's amazement, without looking behind her, the old lady held up her hand. Will froze in the air, unable to move.

"And you wondered why I could possibly be scared of her," Eric's female murmured to Dom.

Dom grinned, and the sight of his smile turned Nev inside out. Hurt, rage and confusion made it hard to think straight.

"Poor bastard." The old woman clucked. "Blondie, up and at 'em."

Dom kissed the human on her forehead before joining Eric. The pair stood next to each other, not three feet from Nev. This close, he could sense their strong bond, as well as a strong human taint mucking the familiarity of what should have smelled like Ravager.

"I'm Gran, not 'old woman'." The old lady interrupted his musings. "Have your piece, do what you need to do, but make it good. Chen's only paying for the concessions because I promised him a show."

Nev glared at Tommy Chen, sitting so calmly by Eric's female and another Ravager scowling his way, his arm possessively around her. Had to be the third in Eric's new pack. Malcolm. A handsome bastard. No wonder Will had been impressed with him.

Unfortunately, he didn't see Kate anywhere, which would upset Will.

"She's far away from here, boy-o," Gran said.

"How did you know—"

"And that 'human bitch' you keep thinking about is my great-granddaughter, Vicki. Your queen, you stupid ass. Pay her some respect."

Nev's jaw dropped open. "We have no queen."

"We haven't until now," Dom answered, his familiar drawl a balm to Nev's loneliness and a scoring pain against the memories he tried to forget.

"But—"

"Could we please get on to the fight? I have things to do tonight," Chen yelled. Several around him tittered while others laughed.

Nev stared hard at Dom and horrified himself by asking, "Why did you leave?"

"You left me long before I left you," Dom answered in a sad but firm voice. "You had a chance to be so much more than your father. Instead, you took the easy way out. Eric rescued me. He saved me from *you*."

Nev slashed out with his claws but missed Eric completely. Savage had gotten faster over the years, damn his *guer* to the Void. "Dom was mine. My pet. He loved *me*."

Eric's eyes flashed. "You abused him; you nearly killed him. Why would he love you for that?"

"I didn't hurt him."

"You had him beaten every day," Eric growled.

"Not me, my father," Nev said, willing Dom to believe him. "I couldn't help his brutality."

Dom looked at him with disgust, his loyalty obviously with Eric. "He was a monster, but so were you. You encouraged him because it made you look strong in his eyes to belittle your poor servant. You blamed me for any and all mistakes *you* made. Instead of standing strong, together, you used me as a scapegoat. A true prime takes responsibility for his actions. A real friend would never have allowed anyone to treat me the way your father did."

Nev allowed that it had been weak to sacrifice Dom the way he had, but he'd needed his father's approval. If Dom had cared about him at all, he would have understood. "Will never complains. None of my clan do. They're all better than any of you Savages."

Turning his attention to Eric, Nev sneered. "And you, what the hell are you?" Nev glared at Vicki, who to his surprise, glared back with a wave of hostile aggression so forceful it was palpable. Shaken, he tried to ignore it. "You take a feeble human as queen? Do you really think she can give you the cubs you so desperately crave? She's a mongrel bitch no better than a whore."

"No, Gran," Vicki shouted. "Let this play out."

The old lady grumbled under her breath and stepped away from them. She sat next to her great-granddaughter and waved at Will, who dropped to the grass, gasping.

"You want a challenge? Bring it," Eric dared. He and Dom stood side by side. Malcolm vaulted over the rail to join them.

"Fine. My pack against yours." He called the men still with him — Will and the dozen Ravagers he commanded.

"Typical." Eric sneered. "Can't face me one-on-one. No matter. We'll kill the rest, then I'll deal with you."

Nev didn't like the surety in Eric's ice-blue eyes. The fuck might very well beat him, especially with Dom and that brute by his side. But he couldn't say no, now, could he?

"So, Chen," he tried, looking for a way out. "I see you've switched sides."

Chen shrugged and waved down a Voider carrying a tray of popcorn. "I never take sides. I just like a good fight." He glanced at Vicki and smiled. To Nev's great satisfaction, she didn't look so brave now. "I'll get what's coming to me. Of that I have no doubt."

Gran chuckled. "Chen's a keeper. Funniest Voider I've ever met. And speaking of funny, there's Sean." She waved and murmured something else to Vicki.

"Enough chatter. Let's get to it." Eric lashed out and connected with Nev's cheek.

Somehow, Savage had gone from clothed and in a man's form into his *guer* in the span of a second. But Nev didn't care how he'd done it. It was time for Eric Savage to die. "Don't kill the blond," he yelled to his men. "He's mine."

Vicki didn't like being on the receiving end of Tommy Chen's full attention. He sparkled with energy, uncomfortable shocks that pricked at her, as if daring her to tangle her energy with his. Full of vitality and stubborn sense, he threatened her on another level entirely. Eric, Dom and Malcolm tempted her. Chen scared her, though she'd be damned if she'd admit it out loud.

She wanted to concentrate on her pack kicking Lawless ass, but Chen scooted nearer on the hard, aluminum bench. Seated a row above him, she should have felt safer than she did, even when he closed the distance between them. And she would have, if Gran hadn't chosen that moment to go get a hotdog.

"Ah, Gran?" she called after the woman.

"Bah, he's not your worry. Mind me, leave off the red sauce. Give you heartburn."

Sometimes her gran made no sense at all.

"So, Vicki," Chen murmured her name, as if savoring it. "I loved watching you fight. Much more entertaining and graceful than Ravagers. They're all brawn, little brain." He raised his glasses to the top of his head, treating her to the dark swirls of energy, deep in his pupils.

"Gee, thanks. Nice to know how you feel about my pack." She felt the insult as her own. Eric and the others were just as smart as Chen. So what if they happened to be big and hairy as well? "How's Mei Lin, by the way?"

"You bruised her pride, not to mention her body, but she's back up and running." They drew silent and watched the Savages pound the snot out of Nev's dregs dirtying up the field. "Where's my ring?" he asked, so silently she almost missed it. But the venom in his voice literally made her cringe.

As one, her pack stopped what they were doing and turned to face her. Not a good thing, since they still had half a dozen Ravagers to take down. She drew her energy in, creating a temporary shield on her emotions. She hoped. She wasn't used to dealing with empathic energy.

"I'm fine!" she yelled at them and pointed at the threat behind them. "Don't turn your backs—"

A mound of limbs, claws and teeth crowded one another. The crowd roared its approval. Trust Eric to give everyone what they wanted. Blood, guts and a lengthy battle, she thought with irritation.

She turned to Chen, annoyed by his wide smile. "Quit threatening me. My pack can feel it. You're interfering with the fight."

"I know. But there are good odds the Savages will win."

"Terrific."

"You have something you want to tell me about my property you stole?" He smiled, the menacing play of humor on his handsome face oddly sensual. He focused on her mouth. "Do you remember our kiss?"

"I'll tell you what I know about your stupid ring," she snapped to stop the direction of Chen's conversation. "But I don't know much."

He said nothing.

Where the hell was Gran?

Vicki sighed. "Well, shit. Look, we at S&V Retrievals pride ourselves on confidentiality and our client's right to whatever they want retrieved."

"It wasn't his to take."

"Hers. Wasn't *hers* to take."

Chen's intensity amped. A subtle flicker of movement on his forearms reminded her of what he'd done at Rock Hall, when she'd first teased him with a kiss. "Explain."

"You're not going to like this, but that ring you think you own belongs to her. Sean and I manipulate energy. Each individual contains a kind of signature, and the more power in a body, the greater the echo that energy leaves behind on certain objects. Sean's pretty good at reading energy signatures. That ring wants to belong to her."

Chen gripped her hand and yanked her close. "Say that again."

"You're hurting me." Despite her fear of the man, she refused to let him get away with strong-arm tactics, not with Ravagers around to witness his show of intimidation.

He blinked and let her go. He even moved back, putting some space between them. "I'm sorry," he said gruffly.

"Don't do it again."

"Don't push me." Hissing sounded from the vicinity of his tattoos, and a spark of green light lit the center of his pupils.

"Ah, right. I had a feeling our client was on the level. But Sean's the one who said the ring wanted to be owned, which really made little sense to me. And sorry, but I can't tell you who our client was. We went through a broker, and even he never saw her face. She met him in a church through the confessional." Great piece of irony there, but she didn't think Chen appreciated it. He looked as if he'd seen a ghost.

"Did you…" He cleared his throat. "Did you happen to see her at all?"

"Just the back of her head once. Long black hair with an almost green tint to it, now that I think about it. I sensed a lot of anger from that brief glimpse. A suppressed rage. Pretty hot, energetically speaking." She was surprised to recall so much from such a short meeting.

She expected anger on Chen's part, frustration that she hadn't given him much.

"So why did she want that ring so badly? Who is she?" Vicki asked to break the sudden silence.

"The ring belonged to her grandfather. A symbol of great power in her family."

So he did know the woman. "And my client?"

"A dead woman who's not so dead." His kiss took her by surprise. This time, however, the alien sense of another man's mouth didn't taste right. "If you weren't already pregnant, I'd throw you over my shoulder and make love to you with thanks. But I've got a promise to keep and my fiancée to find."

"Fiancée?" That poor woman was engaged to Chen? Then what else he'd said dawned on her. "Make love to me? That's your idea of a reward?" Her eyes widened. "Pregnant?" she squeaked, then quickly lowered her voice. "But how — Chen?"

In the blink of an eye, he'd done the impossible. He'd vanished.

Chapter Fourteen

After Chen's announcement, the world around her ceased to exist.

"Told ya, did he?" Gran asked as she sat next to Vicki with two hotdogs in hand. She gave one to Vicki. "Congratulations, honey. And might I say, it's about time. I've been at the end of my rope waiting on this. Finally. Now you're the namesake, not me."

"Gran?"

"Eat. You'll need your strength."

Vicki took a bite to appease her, startled to find she really was hungry.

"I was there when King first stepped into our world. Back when the Voids first opened up, folks were scared of their own shadow. A mass exodus left the less fortunate and the whacked-out humans behind in Cross Step, with the rest of the Voiders. A ton of the Norms in this city are spies for Uncle Sam, you know that? Damn Watchers."

Before her gran could start on the web of conspiracies in Cross Step, Vicki interrupted. "Who's King?"

"The first Ravager Prime to walk in this world. He knew then the problems his kind would have. They can't procreate the way they need to, not without a queen."

Procreate. Pregnant.

"Yep. That'd be you. King's sister told me a long time ago that I'd be the vessel to the line of queens. Have to admit though, I thought it was going to be your aunt before she met Sean Senior. Then when she had a boy, I nearly had a heart attack. Thank God your mother tried again and had you."

Vicki blinked. "You're saying you knew I'd become a Ravager, ah, queen?"

"Had a feeling, but then, I have feelings all the time." Gran waved at Dom and Malcolm watching Eric fight Nev, the last Lawless Ravager still standing. "Take your mates there. Dom's special, has his own brand of power that he'll pass down to your first daughter. And Malcolm's going to be a nightmare when you're carrying his son. He lost his baby brother before coming through the Void. You'll have to help him get over the fear of losing another child."

"What?"

"And Eric." Gran sighed with pleasure. "Prime is going to try to run rings around you. He'll want to settle you, a dominance thing most alphas tend to have. Don't let it worry you. Long as you give as good as you get, you'll rule your pack, as meant. If he tries to snow you with that Prime bullshit, you remind him who's been blessed to carry his twins."

Gran's eyes sparkled.

"Twins?" Vicki felt lightheaded.

"The first set at least. Then after the others, you'll have triplets. Little monsters, sorry to say. Gonna give you fits unless you spank them. It's not your fault, really, but a combination of Ravager and Morely genes are going to turn your kids into really powerful little beasts. I'm hoping to live long enough to see more than the twins, but we'll see."

Gran had never been able to predict the deaths of anyone in her family. Then again, she'd never been so forthcoming with what she knew before.

Vicki had a hard time wrapping her head around it. "But, but... Three husbands? Mates? They're not human, Gran," she whispered harshly.

Gran whispered back, "Neither are you." In a louder voice, she added with a chuckle, "Don't be so stubborn. You have men who love you. What could possibly be wrong with your situation? Not as if you don't have strong feelings for them, is it?"

She opened her mouth to reject the idea but couldn't.

Gran smirked. "Thought so. Now you're going to give rise to a new generation of Ravagers. You'll be the perfect queen they need, Vicki. A new namesake." Gran's eyes shone with happy tears. "Name your first girl Vicki, okay? For me."

"I love you, Gran." Vicki hugged her great-grandmother, understanding so much more, now.

"I love you too, sweet. Well, would you look at that? The Lawless prime is no more. Pity they let Will live though. That's going to bite them in the ass later." Gran dashed the tears from her eyes as she started on a fight commentary that amused everyone around them.

Vicki tried to process it all, but the best she could do when her mates left the field, bloodied and battered, was to demand they return home.

* * * * *

Eric didn't know what to think. Once back at the compound outside the city, he felt that he could at least breathe again. His clan celebrated their victory with his grateful permission. Tomorrow he'd make sure to round up the Lawless Ravagers still skulking about the border and offer them the chance to join the Savages or die. He still didn't like letting Will live, but Dom had insisted. Stupid foresight.

Tonight should have been one big party. Instead, Vicki and Dom moped as if they'd lost something. Dom, he could understand. His guard had a past with Nev, and no matter that it hadn't been pretty, with Nev's death, one more piece of Ravager history departed this world. Nev was the last in an ancient line of Ravagers, one that would never be known again.

Good riddance. But Eric didn't say that to Dom. Instead, he left Malcolm with his somber guard in their room. He continued past the revelers, searching for the *guer* that had entwined with his not so long ago. He sensed Vicki before Rule pointed to a dimly lit path leading to a secret garden several of the females had a hand in tending.

Vicki stood over a rosebush, staring without seeing at the receding bloom.

"Okay, that's it." Eric glared at her, pleased when she jumped and glared back. He much preferred her angry than sad, and it bothered him that he couldn't seem to take care of her issue. "What the hell is your problem?"

"My problem?" she repeated, her voice dangerously quiet.

He tried to temper his arousal, but her fury prodded his desire.

"Just a few days ago I was a woman working for a successful firm living a successful life."

"A dangerous life," he muttered, still not liking the thought of Tommy Chen anywhere near her. When he'd felt her fear in that football stadium, it had taken all his energy not to go to her when she denied needing him. Chen bothered her and thus the Voider bothered him.

"But it was my life." The angry tears in her eyes froze him to the spot.

"Vicki, baby, don't—"

"Don't tell me not to cry." She glared at him, and he felt a surge of energy immobilize his legs. By the Void, her power made her so incredibly sexy. "I can do all sorts of things now. Fuck!" Then she said a few other things, stunning him.

He'd never heard her swear so much in such a short span of time. And then he realized she'd been rubbing her belly while standing in front of the roses. He felt the blood rush from his head.

"Vicki?" he said hoarsely. "Is there anything you want to tell me?" Dom's blond head appeared behind Vicki at the mouth of the trail, followed closely by Malcolm. A subtle wave kept them both back.

"Yeah, I have something to tell you, you big jerk. I'm pregnant with *puppies*," she snarled. "You kidnapped me, you bullied me, and somehow—because God knows I have no clue how it happened—you made me fall in love with you and the other two idiots pretending to be invisible behind me."

The large grin splitting Dom's sober face thrilled him.

Vicki was carrying his babe—babes. Eric wanted to howl with joy.

But Vicki wouldn't let anyone move. Her anger was a thing of beauty as she took it out on the three of them. "I have a life, you know. And now I'm stuck with three Ravagers who know shit about romance, shit about how to treat an independent woman and shit about love."

"What do you mean, stuck? You should be honored to be chosen to serve as queen," he said to stir her wrath. He needed a moment to gather his emotions. To his shock, he felt his heart shatter and fall at her feet and had to blink back tears of pride and happiness. And horror. This grand affection, this *love*, he felt for the woman would be his undoing. Like the other females in his clan, she'd soon learn she ruled the pack. Talk about a nightmare.

Dom and Malcolm shared a wide-assed grin before Dom said, "Eric, I told you. Humans are different."

Malcolm smirked at Eric before blinking his big brown eyes at their mate. "Vicki, *I* love you."

She opened her mouth then snapped it closed. "What?"

"Since you first knocked me out. You're stubborn, beautiful and your *guer* is the most powerful force of feminine energy I've ever experienced. Remember, I felt you in the forest, when you helped me defeat that Lawless pack. I believe what I feel for you is the equivalent of human love." He looked too nervous to be a six-and-a-half-foot predator. Mangy bastard. Malcolm was trying to win Vicki over with a false show of vulnerability.

For fuck's sake. It was working!

Vicki smiled through tears and let him gather her up in his arms.

"We can't know what love is," Dom added in a quiet voice. "But we feel it all the same. Why do you think I told our prime to mark you? Because I felt it even then." He whispered something to her Eric couldn't hear.

The blasted woman pulled Dom to her and hugged him tight.

Then the three of them turned to him.

"What?"

"Out with it," Vicki demanded. Hell, she even growled like a proper mate. *His queen.*

His gaze centered on her belly, and he licked his lips. "Puppies, eh?"

She narrowed her eyes. "Eric Savage. I want to hear it."

"Actually, they're Ravagers." He focused and smiled with satisfaction. "Two of them." *My sons.* He studied his pack and amended, *our* sons.

"Eric?" Her yellow eyes blazed with anger, with love and with an uncertainty that made his teasing no longer amusing.

"Hell, Vicki. You're the only female I've ever marked. The only one who can tie my balls in a knot with one look."

"*That's* what you have to say to me?" her voice was almost shrill.

Damn if she wouldn't pull it from him, word by word. "Shit, Vicki. You're the only woman who can scare the hell out of me. The thought of you in danger stirs my *guer* to a frenzy. When you're mad, you set me on fire. I can't think of anything but fucking you senseless, and then you have me fucking *them* senseless." He nodded to Dom and Malcolm, who stared at him in fascination.

"Vicki, I'm yours," he admitted through gritted teeth, trying not to wince at the large grin of triumph on her face. "Our *guers* are tied. There's no going back. *You're mine*," he roared to the heavens. "You, Dom and Malcolm belong to me. I claimed you, dammit. You're not going anywhere, and I'll never give you up, not any of you," he said, a warning to Malcolm who was too new to the pack to know better.

As she and the others closed the distance between them, Eric saw his mistake. It wasn't triumph on her face, but that same love she professed to want so badly from him.

"You love me," she challenged. "You just don't want to admit it."

He swallowed hard, his gaze going from her eyes to her belly, to Dom and Malcolm, practically glowing with affection. A surge of protectiveness, of warmth, desire, *of love*, pushed past his resistance. What could three little words hurt, anyway?

"I love you." He liked the way her eyes filled even as she tried to scowl at him. "Happy now?" he growled, totally claimed by this woman.

"Yes, as a matter of fact I am," she growled back, then smiled with such evil delight he couldn't contain a groan. "You're mine, he's mine and he's mine," she said, pointing at them all. "I'm claiming all of you. It's official." Devious enjoyment made his *guer* shake under the force of her love. "That means you're mine, now, wolfie."

Dom chuckled. Malcolm grinned.

"Ah, Vicki? You think I could have my legs back now?" Eric was forced to ask.

She blinked in astonishment, waved his legs free, then leapt into his arms.

He crushed her to him, never planning to let her go.

"Wolfie?" Malcolm laughed. "So what's my nickname? I prefer Stud or Big Man."

"Don't encourage her," Dom chided, his smile wide enough to split his handsome face. "I told you, Prime. She's yours."

"Yeah," Eric agreed. He'd never felt as complete as he did right now. "You're right, as always. My woman, my queen. My mates," he said with satisfaction, looking at the three of them.

Vicki kissed him until he could think of nothing more than getting inside her. She broke off to take Dom's mouth, then Malcolm's. "I don't know if I mentioned it, but I'm a bit perverted myself. I can't wait to see you two molest Malcolm again. He's so pretty, isn't he? Almost as pretty as Dom."

They laughed, and Vicki moaned into Eric's next kiss.

"Wait," she whispered on a breath. "What about the others? Sean, and Logan and Jesse? Are they okay?"

Dom stroked the side of her face. "Sean and Diana are fine. As for Logan and Jesse…"

Malcolm tried to stifle a snort but failed.

"Malcolm?" Eric frowned. "What don't I know?"

"Kate's in over her head with those two. I heard what they had planned. All this talk of females claiming males, well, in their case, I think it's going to be the other way around."

"You mean, the way *I* claimed Vicki and you two? The way *I'm* in charge?" Eric teased.

"In your dreams, Prime," Vicki muttered and unbuttoned his shirt, sliding her warm hands up and down his skin.

Dom got to work on Eric's trousers, and Malcolm reached a hand between Eric and Vicki to encircle his cock.

Eric groaned and kissed her again, enthralled with his pack. "Always in my dreams, Vicki. So long as they're of the three of you," he breathed before returning kisses among his mates.

It was a long time before any of them returned to the house.

Also by Marie Harte

eBooks:
Kate Undone
Namesake

About the Author

Marie Harte is a professed bibliophile with an addiction to romance. She's fond of things that go bump in the night, especially if they happen to be tall, dark and handsome. Life has given her some interesting insights into the male mind. After majoring in English, she spent several years in the Marine Corps, followed by stints in information technology, logistics and the transportation fields. And yes, herding cats is easier then trying to manage truck drivers.

Now a wife, writer and crazy woman with children, she spends most of her time bugging her kids to do their homework while typing with a mad zeal to make deadlines. She's a multi-published and bestselling author of erotic romance who's obsessed with email, so feel free to drop her a line.

Marie welcomes comments from readers. You can find her website and email address on her author bio page at www.ellorascave.com.

Tell Us What You Think

We appreciate hearing reader opinions about our books. You can email us at Comments@EllorasCave.com.

Why an electronic book?

We live in the Information Age—an exciting time in the history of human civilization, in which technology rules supreme and continues to progress in leaps and bounds every minute of every day. For a multitude of reasons, more and more avid literary fans are opting to purchase e-books instead of paper books. The question from those not yet initiated into the world of electronic reading is simply: *Why?*

1. *Price.* An electronic title at Ellora's Cave Publishing and Cerridwen Press runs anywhere from 40% to 75% less than the cover price of the exact same title in paperback format. Why? Basic mathematics and cost. It is less expensive to publish an e-book (no paper and printing, no warehousing and shipping) than it is to publish a paperback, so the savings are passed along to the consumer.

2. *Space.* Running out of room in your house for your books? That is one worry you will never have with electronic books. For a low one-time cost, you can purchase a handheld device specifically designed for e-reading. Many e-readers have large, convenient screens for viewing. Better yet, hundreds of titles can be stored within your new library—on a single microchip. There are a variety of e-readers from different manufacturers. You can also read e-books on your PC or laptop computer. (Please note that Ellora's Cave does not endorse any specific brands.

You can check our websites at www.ellorascave.com or www.ccrridwenpress.com for information we make available to new consumers.)

3. *Mobility.* Because your new e-library consists of only a microchip within a small, easily transportable e-reader, your entire cache of books can be taken with you wherever you go.

4. *Personal Viewing Preferences.* Are the words you are currently reading too small? Too large? Too... ANNOYING? Paperback books cannot be modified according to personal preferences, but e-books can.

5. *Instant Gratification.* Is it the middle of the night and all the bookstores near you are closed? Are you tired of waiting days, sometimes weeks, for bookstores to ship the novels you bought? Ellora's Cave Publishing sells instantaneous downloads twenty-four hours a day, seven days a week, every day of the year. Our webstore is never closed. Our e-book delivery system is 100% automated, meaning your order is filled as soon as you pay for it.

Those are a few of the top reasons why electronic books are replacing paperbacks for many avid readers.

As always, Ellora's Cave and Cerridwen Press welcome your questions and comments. We invite you to email us at Comments@ellorascave.com or write to us directly at Ellora's Cave Publishing Inc., 1056 Home Avenue, Akron, OH 44310-3502.

Make each day more *EXCITING* With our

Ellora's Cavemen Calendar

www.EllorasCave.com

Discover for yourself why readers can't get enough of the multiple award-winning publisher Ellora's Cave.

Whether you prefer e-books or paperbacks, be sure to visit EC on the web at www.ellorascave.com

for an erotic reading experience that will leave you breathless.

Made in the USA
Lexington, KY
14 April 2011